Tempest

I've seen pictures of his house, of course I have. We traveled together for a year, backpacking across the world. He became my closest friend and confidant. He's the best person I know, which is what brings me to now as I stand here, looking at his bloody beach house! It's like something Barbie would live in except it's not pink.

How can Mad be such a cool person when he came from all of this money? It's insane. The pictures he showed me make the place look a lot smaller than it actually is, but he's very good at photography. I bet he did it on purpose.

"Not one to brag are you, Mad?" I grin at my friend as he climbs out of the black Uber and opens the boot of the car. "You weren't lying when you said there'd be space."

He nudges me with his shoulder, looking embarrassed by it all, and slings both my heavy backpack and his onto his shoulders. "Come on. Let's see if Dad's home."

I trail behind a little, taking in the scenery, it's hot here, nearly as hot as India but not quite. India's heat is a bit dryer but more powerful. This is a bit more humid, probably because we're on the coast and there's a nice breeze to take the edge off.

The breezy places are killer though, because you don't feel your skin burning until it's too late. I need to lather on my factor fifty before leaving the house.

I can't believe I'm staying here.

When he opens the door, I yank on the bobble at the back of his curly, dark hair. He needs a trim but he won't. He's growing it until he can chop it off for a cause. Nothing that Mad does is for selfish gain.

"Leave my hair, Pest," he snaps playfully, his eyes twinkling with humor as he kicks the bottom of the door. "Get the handle."

I yank it down, trying to peek through the glass on either side but loose voile covers them, making it hard to see much but a spacious hall. This is confirmed when we step inside.

I feel so out of place and funnily enough, I can tell Mad does too.

"Beats that shack in Cambodia," I mutter and bend down to undo the laces of my walking boots.

"Leave them," Mad says, dropping our bags on the floor next to a white door which I'm guessing is a closet. "DAD?"

This place is so big, his voice echoes. I've never seen such high ceilings in a home before. In fancy hotels and such, yes, but not homes. I bet it costs a fortune to keep cool.

"I told him we wouldn't be here until four, so he might not be home yet." He looks around anxiously and I can tell he's missed his dad.

"Why?"

HIS
FATHER

A. E. MURPHY

Zean Maskell, this one is yours. I hope you like it but if you don't, I still love you.

He scrunches up his nose, making his plump upper lip seem thicker. "I got the timeline confused."

"Now why doesn't that surprise me?" I laugh and grab my bag. "I really need a sho—"

"Maddox?" A deep, male voice echoes over the sound of a door sliding open somewhere beyond the long hall. I can't wait to tour this place.

I'm anxious to meet his dad, I've seen a picture of him smiling with Mad on his shoulders when he was a young boy. I didn't inspect it thoroughly and now I really wish I had.

As his father rounds the corner, where the hallway opens up on the right at the very end, my breathing stops. My eyes are likely as round as saucers and I genuinely forget to breathe.

He's... gorgeous.

He has thick brows, those are the first thing I notice, but they're thick in the way everybody wants their eyebrows to be thick. They shadow sky-blue orbs that have a powerful dark ring of midnight around the striking edges. I want to paint them, I want to stare into them and capture every fleck of color, every genetic imperfection of his iris and pointed pupils. Thick, long lashes cast a shade onto his lower lids which only make the color pop more. Mad has similar eyes, I think, but nowhere near as striking as this.

I'm staring. I can't help myself.

He has dimples that are slowly vanishing as his smile becomes a frown and his frown becomes a scowl in my direction.

"Dad, meet Pest," Maddox introduces me, placing a hand on my elbow. "Pest, this is my dad, Sargent."

3

I already knew his name but I pretend I didn't and extend a hand which could be cleaner, but in my defense, we just traveled for eight hours from Cambodia to LA and there are no showers on airplanes the last I checked.

"This is Pest?" Sargent looks at his son, his blue eyes glowing with confusion and ire as he ignores my hand and lets it hang between us. This is awkward.

Uh-oh.

"She's a girl."

"I did clear that up in my last email, Dad, before you said she could stay." Maddox frowns, dropping his bag again and squaring up to his father who has maybe a hundred pounds more of muscle on his frame. He's wearing shorts and a vest, I can see everything, including the sharp point tribal tattoo peeking over his right shoulder. I wonder how big it is and where it leads. "Did you read the emails or did you just have Marcy do it for you?"

"I didn't read them all, I wanted you to tell me your tales when you arrived," he snaps, giving me another look, this one even less pleasant than the last. His eyes drag from my dirty boots to my messy hair which still has mud and Lord knows what else in it.

I'm wearing a very baggy checked shirt and leggings that I cut above the knees. They're comfy and not too warm, and cheap to replace when they are no longer wearable. It's safe to say I look like I just crawled out of Oxfam and not Prada.

"I'm sorry if me staying is a burden," I input quickly before the situation escalates. "If I could just get cleaned up and rest a while I'll be on my way." I don't want to stay where I'm not welcome but I don't have anywhere else to go right now. Not because I feel intimidated by this man but because I'm not a pushover and I can see me not getting on with him despite him being my host. I'll never be anything but polite so long as that attitude is returned.

Quiet I may be, pushover I am not.

"You're not going anywhere," Mad snaps, looking, well, mad. "Dad." He cuts his father with a glare. "You're being a douchebag."

I'm glad he said it because I was thinking it.

"I know, I'm sorry." He pushes his short hair back and looks at me before extending a hand.

I take it but only after a nudge from Mad. I wanted to leave him hanging like he just did for me. I'm that level of petty.

His large hand engulfs mine and squeezes gently. "You're welcome to stay for the length agreed."

His meaning isn't lost on me. He means the length agreed and not a second more.

I should have insisted on speaking with his father before even entertaining the idea of coming all the way to Malibu. I should have tried to form a relationship with him before arriving. I'm an idiot.

When he releases my hand, he turns to his son and they hug at last. "It's good to see you, Maddox."

"You too."

"We'll have dinner together tonight, I'll have Marcy book us a table."

"Not tonight." Mad pulls back. "We've been flying for eight

hours and three kids were screaming the entire ride. Plus, jet lag, you know?"

"Of course." He smiles so warmly at his son I almost start to like him. I almost start to find him attractive again. "I'll leave you both to rest for tonight and accost you in the morning."

"Thank you for having me, Sarge," I say, and his eyes narrow on me infinitesimally.

"It's Sargent, or Mr. Wolf."

Yikes. He's super intense.

Though again, I'm not intimidated because I'm trying not to laugh at his name, Sargent Wolf.

"*Dad*," Mad snaps, grabbing his bag and then my arm. "Come on, Pest. I'll show you where you'll be sleeping."

Sargent

He's finally home, after nearly a year away. I hated the thought I'd have to share him with a friend but said yes purely because I knew if I'd said no, he would have delayed his journey longer.

Had I known his friend would be female I'd have let the journey delay. Though knowing Maddox, he would have simply shown up with her anyway. The stubborn shit that he is.

Why didn't I read the emails? I saw the pictures but they were always group photos. I didn't pay attention to the filthy little dark-haired harlot in his photos.

It was obvious they were close but so was everybody in the pictures he sent. He's very good at photography. He likely did it that way knowing I'd miss it and say yes, knowing Marcy would also manipulate the situation so I can't say no. I'm not a complete bastard, not always. I just can't stand the thought of a woman in my house for days and nights on end. Filling the space with her *things*, her scent, her *womanly* touch.

Tampons in the bathroom, hair in the drains, nail polish on the sides of the basin. I dealt with that fucking crap once for his psycho of a mother, never again.

Nonetheless, I was raised better than how I behaved. I'm a grown man and I likely frightened the little girl to death. Not that she showed it in her defiant little shortening of my name. I loathe being called Sarge nearly as much as I loathe having a woman in my home.

Soon my son leads her away and she pierces me with a curious look over her shoulder. Those round, warm, greenish-hazel, innocent eyes narrow with intrigue.

I wait for them to enter the spare room before I follow. My apology is stuck in my throat, rehearsed and ready though I don't mean it, not fully. I'm only saying it so Maddox doesn't give me a hard time, which I know he will.

The door is still open, I can hear their voices drifting my way. Hers is hushed so I can't make out what she's saying but his isn't.

"My dad is scarred," he explains and I have to lean on the wall with my hand for support. "My mom did a number on us both. He never got over it. Never learned to trust again."

"He never moved on?" Her voice is louder now and her meaning is clear. She thinks I'm some virginal little martyr, waiting for the right woman. Ha. The thought is laughable.

"Oh, no, I wouldn't say that. He's always with somebody, but never here. It's always just been me and him, and his assistant, Marcy, who was originally male when my dad hired her, so she doesn't count."

"You've told me about Marcy, she sounds amazing."

"She is, my dad would be lost without her."

I would not.

"Just give him time and ignore him if he's rude. He doesn't mean it. He's just scarred. Badly, badly, scarred."

I am not scarred. I just can't be dealing with the same fake bitch trashing my life day in, day out when I can have my pick, day in, day out. Who needs the rest of the baggage when you can choose between every pussy letter of the alphabet?

"You might have told me this about your dad before, though."

I hear my son sigh and my chest tightens. "I thought he'd be better than that. His email seemed so sincere but, then, I should have known it wasn't him who sent it."

Fuck.

I back away quietly, deciding my apologies are better suited for the morning.

He's also wrong, I'm not still holding onto the pain of what his mother did or any morbid shit like that. I'm simply enjoying life this way, without the influence of a woman.

I guess I shouldn't blame my son for wanting a woman in his life. He'll soon learn to stay away. There's something about this girl, something in her eyes that I don't like. She's going to be hard work.

Tempest

I can't believe this house. It's insane.

Everything is glass, every room has floor-to-ceiling windows overlooking an incredible view of Malibu. We're high up so nobody can see in without trespassing first. Everything is the same color, the floors are all a brownish, gray wood that's glossy and gorgeous. The walls are an off white with cleverly placed art here and there. The furniture is minimal but so comfy looking and classy.

Mad only gave me a brief tour last night as we were both wiped but he told me to make myself at home. I'm not sure I can, not until I've spoken to his father and cleared the air. As much as I'd like to make myself scarce immediately I am stuck here until I can make alternative arrangements. He agreed to have me so he will have to deal with it. I was just calling his bluff in the hall yesterday when we arrived, knowing on the spot he wouldn't have told me to fuck off because Mad would have followed.

It's such a shame that such a handsome man is such an arse.

I stretch on the rug in my bedroom after a second, long, hot shower. It's been so long since I felt the softness of a shaggy rug. Especially one so expensive and authentic.

My wet hair dampens it as I stare at the ceiling in a pair of Mad's gray boxer briefs and a white vest that's a bit too large. All of my things need cleaning. Not that I have many things. This is why I had a shower before bed and one upon waking, I was filthy. Now I feel clean, so squeaky clean. It's amazing. I never want to feel dirty again.

I unravel the leather strap from around my journal and roll onto my front. The sun is only now rising outside but my mind's jet lag had it rising two hours ago and in Cambodia we always got up before it broke through the darkness anyway. We had to, to gather water from a mile away and have it filtered and ready to drink.

I write:

"Today is going to be a good day, I can feel it. Today is a day of harmony and happiness and today I'll try to bond with Sargent. I still can't believe Mad told Marcy to purposely withhold the fact I'm female, just so I could come here with him. I knew he valued my friendship and company but to the extent that he'd risk the wrath of his father just to keep me around is mind blowing."

I roll my journal back up and tuck it under my pillow after I stand, stretch again, check my thick braid that hangs over my left shoulder, and then I exit my bedroom.

The polite thing to do would be to wait for Maddox to wake up but I am starving and he put my bag in the utility room with his. I have maybe two meal replacement bars in the front pocket that I forgot to take out before handing it over.

I creep along the hall, keeping to the right as I make my way to the large archway that joins the hallway to the open-plan kitchen and dining room, which also leads to the most amazing outdoor pool I have ever seen. It looks like you can swim straight over the side. I've never seen anything like it.

Sure beats the piranha-infested waters we dared to swim in. Maddox even got bitten once, that wasn't fun. Nasty little gits they can be. He still has the scar to prove it above his right ankle bone.

On bare feet and tiptoes I move silently across the kitchen and through another door, relieved when I see my bag on the side where Mad left it, though it's empty of clothing and the washing machine is making a racket. He must have chucked our shoes in there with our clothes. Not an uncommon thing to do when backpacking but definitely not the right thing to do in normal civilization.

I laugh quietly and peel open the meal replacement bar. It leaves much to be desired in the flavor department but I'm starving. This is the first thing I have eaten since that awful plane meal that I took one bite of yesterday.

Sargent

"What are you doing?" I bark and she startles, squealing like a little girl as she spins to face me. There's something hanging from between her lips, something in a silver packet. She grabs it and swallows the piece in her mouth.

"Getting food," she replies, placing her hand to her heart and my eyes, unfortunately, catch sight of her perky rosebud nipples that are clearly visible through the white tank top she's donning.

Damn it, she has amazing breasts. I bet they'd be heavy in my hands despite their perkiness and I'm almost certain the shape I see surrounding the pebbled tip of her left nipple is a piercing.

Why do I like that?

She shifts on the spot, uncomfortable by my staring and now I feel like a perverted fool.

I look at her in the eyes and keep my expression flat despite the raging hard-on my pants are hopefully concealing.

"Eating what?" I ask. She's my son's girl. I am sick. Or I am normal for appreciating a beautiful female form, which she definitely has. Gentle curves, if not a bit too slender from her travels, perky breasts which I can't stop looking at, wider hips than most of the women I'm used to fucking in Malibu. I bet she has a great ass.

I have to stop myself from leaning around to check it out.

"It's a meal replacement thing, like a cereal bar. It's supposed to be beef dinner flavor but it tastes like shit actually."

She just swore, my cock, which is already fucking killing me, gives a happy little twitch. I don't typically speak to women with a potty mouth, I think I might like that too. Piercings and curse words... what an odd thing to enjoy.

"Why are you eating *shit* in my laundry room?" I frown,

12

crossing my arms over my chest. A strike of manly satisfaction courses through me when she looks at my own assets. For an older man I've still got it, as I should, I work hard for this body and eat right.

"I'm hungry," she replies as though I'm stupid as she pushes a hand through her hair, showing me a black and gray, surprisingly beautiful tattoo on her arm. It's a swirling pattern with roses and hidden faces that has been so artistically done. I pull my eyes away because staring at her isn't helping my arousal.

I fucking love tasteful tattoos on women and this one, which spans from her shoulder to her elbow, is gorgeous.

"There is a refrigerator full of food."

Her lips twitch when I say refrigerator. Is she mocking me in her mind? Like she can mock anyone with her common-sounding British accent that is probably fake anyway.

"I'm not the type to make myself at home when my host is less than pleased to see me," she admits, straight to the point of the issue, I like that. I might just respect her a little more for it.

"I apologize for my less than adequate greeting yesterday, allow me to redeem myself in the form of eggs benedict and toast."

She smiles happily, stretching her dark pink lips which I think are their natural color. What a lucky, stunning young woman. My son certainly has good taste. She is a beauty.

I allow myself one more act of perversion and move to the side so she has to walk past me and I get to see her delectable derriere as she goes. It's even better than I imagined. And now, I must put all of that out of my head and treat her like the son-stealing harlot that she is.

"Have you ever had eggs benedict?" I ask, moving to the refrigerator and pulling it open.

"Nope," she replies, pulling herself up onto the counter.

I'm torn between ogling her bare thighs or following the pretty glow of her tan to her feet and back up to her cunt. I wonder if, when she slides down, the boxers will hug her lips like a glove and show me just a glimpse of her young pussy.

How old is she anyway? If she's my son's age she's far too young for my perverted mind. Even though she looks all woman. Her body is that of an athlete in her mid-twenties at the latest and I can't stop obsessing.

"There are stools," I snap, my anger misplaced.

"Sorry, Sarge." She hops down. I grit my teeth at the sound of that name. "It's a habit. You just sort of sit wherever you can when you're backpacking."

I light the stove and get to work making breakfast, turning on the radio to fill the silence and to stop me from having to speak with her for any longer.

Tempest

He places a full plate in front of me and my stomach growls its approval. I hope he doesn't hear it over the music.

"Thank you." I politely bow my head and bring my hand up to touch my hair.

"Something you learned in Cambodia?"

I nod and reply, "A custom in a village I was in a while ago,

14

a habit you learned quickly or you quickly felt a cane strike your bare thighs." He shifts on the spot and I wonder if I've made him uncomfortable. "It's a habit you don't forget once you feel the pain of that thin piece of polished wood when it hits you."

His dark eyes stare at me for the longest moment and then he takes his plate and leaves the kitchen without another word, vanishing into the hall.

Was it something I said?

Moments later Maddox sleepily enters. "Dad's been cooking?"

I nod, smiling at his nest of messy hair. Yanking the amber beads that dangle around his neck I admonish, "You shouldn't sleep in those. It's dangerous."

He hits my hand away and rolls his eyes. "Sorry, Mom."

I finish my breakfast as he helps himself to what's left in the pan.

"What did my dad say to you?"

"He just offered me breakfast." And he ogled my body in a way that was so obvious and degrading I wanted to kick him in his nuts. Not that I don't appreciate the attention of a good-looking man, but not one that so obviously disrespects me based on the fact I have a vagina. Which, by the straining in his trousers, he wants to plunder with his cock.

He's Maddox's dad. It's just wrong on so many levels. I mean, Maddox is twenty-one, so he has to be at least forty, that's *if* he was a young father. He doesn't look old, but he does look handsomely mature. Why do handsome men age so well? I deduct he can't be older than forty-three.

"Good." He takes a bite of his eggs and moans. "I've missed being home."

"I'm not surprised, look at this place." I grin, swinging my arms out. "It's amazing. What does your dad do and can I do it too?"

"He runs a transportations company. He handles imports and exports for some pretty major businesses all around the world."

I nod slowly, impressed. "He runs it?"

"With my godfather, yep. They started when they were in their teens and worked hard to build something together."

"That's inspirational."

He shrugs and smiles sheepishly. "He missed out on a lot though, building his empire. It's why he's so lax with me. He wants me to experience life before I tie myself to his company."

"That's actually really nice. I wish I had parents like that."

His hand squeezes my knee when I tilt my head and spy a fancy-looking camera inside a kitchen cupboard, through a glass panel.

"One of yours?"

"No." He puffs out his cheeks. "That's my dad's. He keeps it there for the memories because he doesn't get the urge anymore. When he was younger he wanted to be a photographer. He's the one who taught me all about lighting and angles."

"Is he good?"

"He's incredible. He has an eye for images. He never took random shots, even as I was growing up. Every shot was perfect." He looks to be awed by his own opinions. He really

16

respects and loves his dad. And then he ruins it by smirking while saying, "But I surpassed him quickly enough."

"Humble," I giggle, yanking on his necklace again. "Do you think he'll let me draw him naked?"

Maddox chokes on a laugh and pretends to vomit. "You're not... digging him, are you?"

"Ew, I mean, no, he's nice to look at and I've got literally every other body shape drawn. Your dad is like, *all* muscle."

He shudders. "I'm staying out of this one, I can guarantee it'll be a definite no."

I try to hide my disappointment but it sucks because it's all for the art.

"Besides, I'm all muscle!" Maddox declares, flexing his biceps.

"Yeah, but I already drew you and he's twice your muscle size." Well, he's bigger but not twice as big. "It's good you follow his workout regime and a shame you don't pay attention to his good sense of hair styling."

Feigning offense, he shoves me so hard I stumble off the stool and fall onto my side. We both laugh until I kick his stool out from under him and he joins me on the floor. I screech and scramble on the wooden surface to get away when he grabs my braid and digs his fingers into my sides.

"No!" I laugh so hard I can't breathe, he's relentless. He doesn't stop, pinning me by straddling my chest. "UNCLE!"

He finally stops, climbs off me and offers me a hand as I pant and gasp for breath. I take it and let him pull me to standing. I slap his chest for good measure.

"Morning." Sargent enters the room with his empty plate.

"Sorry for being rude, I had to make a call, are you hungry, Maddox?"

"No," Mad replies, still beaming. He rubs his hip, the one that he landed on when I kicked the stool out from under him. "I'm okay. The leftovers were epic."

"Good."

"When do you want me to start work?" he asks. "The sooner I have a steady income the better."

As Sargent replies I take our plates to the sink and figure out the weird tap with a shower head that you can move around, I'm assuming it's to rinse the plates off. I like it.

"We have a dishwasher," Sargent snaps, no longer talking about getting his son on his own team. "That really isn't necessary."

"It's three plates and a pan," I reply, looking at the dishwasher door and yanking it open. As expected it's empty.

"Dad." Maddox clicks his fingers to get his father's glowering eyes off me. "Work?"

Sargent

"You can start Thursday," I reply. "But don't think we'll go easy on you because you're my son." I look at our *guest*. Her presence alone infuriates me. "Will you be getting a job?"

"I actually already have one," she responds, smiling sheepishly and my son looks at her with such adoration.

"Really?" I am intrigued. "Doing what?"

"I'll be starting at that diner near the freeway on Saturday."

"Bill's Space?" I ask and I look at my son who still has that look in his eye. Boy does he have it bad.

"She's also an incredible painter and even better at drawing." Maddox twirls a lock of her hair around his finger. I'm not sure he realizes he's doing it.

"But please don't worry, I won't use any paints or anything in your house," she blurts, looking sideways at my son.

"We'll find a space for you," Maddox offers, turning away from me completely. "Maybe in the yard. Right, Dad?"

I don't reply. As much as I appreciate art, finding her a space will just entice her to stay.

My phone ringing saves me from replying. I walk away, trying not to think about the visual she planted in my mind, of a cane hitting her tanned skin.

3

Tempest

This morning when I read the note on the counter, the one wishing me the best of luck at my first day of work, I had thought it would bring me the luck it wished for me. I was wrong. Today was hard, so hard. The diner in question is busy, extremely busy, and I just can't wrap my head around this payment system. Two dollars an hour and the rest in tips? I hardly made fifty quid for ten hours' work. People in such a rich area of the state are tight with their tips.

I mean, yeah, okay, I get that I'm new and I made a few mistakes but still.

Plus, the other women who work there are cliquey and bitchy and kept taking my tables.

Still, I grinned and got on with it. My new boss, Bill himself, who gave me the job over email after taking pity of my circumstances, told me he was impressed with how hard I worked and gave me a welcome bonus. That brought me up to seventy dollars for ten hours of nonstop work. I got lunch too, so it wasn't so bad.

Bill seems like a nice guy, a bit overweight and breathless, and a bit sweaty smelling but I could tell he had his heart in the right place.

Besides, I worked for less in Cambodia and Thailand, I guess I was just hoping to have a bit more to put away. Never mind. I'm moaning because I'm tired.

I knock on the door and push it open then immediately go to my room before anybody can see the state of me. My hair is a frizzy mess, falling out of the bun that was neatly made this morning. My eye makeup is smudged, my face pale from exhaustion, and nausea from eating an extremely greasy burger. I haven't had something so greasy and heavy in so long, it's not sitting right. There was little else on the menu though but tomorrow I'll try harder to find something. Perhaps a baked potato.

When I enter my bedroom, I smile when I see a top and matching bottom on the bed, made from soft black material, with another note like the one this morning.

It reads:

Congratulations on finishing your first day. M.

I didn't have anything to swim in and I expressed my need to go shopping as soon as I got my first round of cash. Cash which I can now tuck away in my underwear drawer because Maddox has treated me. It makes me feel bad for not getting him anything on his first day of work which, from what I've heard, he excelled at. I knew he would. He's been groomed his entire life to help his dad. I wish I had a dad who cared enough about my future to help me learn anything.

There's a knock on the door.

Sargent

Maddox stands when he hears the front door open and close, signifying the end of the girl's first day of work, leaving me to my thoughts and paperwork. Clearly, he's had enough of invoices and wage slips. Even though I have a team of financial gurus, I still want him to know how to do things. Should anything happen to me I need to know he's capable of handling all aspects of our company.

I stack the paperwork in order and then stretch and close my eyes, if only to listen to the blissful silence I haven't had yet today. It's like meditation but without the humming and the crossing of legs.

I roll my eyes when I hear the girl's sharp scream. It pierces my peace and I want to cane her myself for it.

It has been four days and that visual is still in my head.

"Must you?" I snarl aggressively when Maddox comes running through the room moments later in swimming trunks.

The female in question is on his back, her bare legs wrapped around his waist, her slender arms around his neck.

He runs past me at the dining table and straight through the open sliding doors.

She screams again when he launches them into the pool sideways and they hit the water with a loud splash that leaves them both spluttering and laughing.

I slam the door closed and stalk to my room. Noise, so much noise.

When I return an hour later for food, Maddox is standing in the kitchen with a towel around his waist, carefully placing food onto three plates from a glass dish.

"What have you made?" I ask, remembering how happy I am to see him home. Though I wonder, with the salary he'll soon be making, how long will he stay before he gets his own place with little Miss Charity Case?

"Baked salmon and sweet potato fries with vegetables, nothing fancy."

"Sounds great."

He smiles at me over his shoulder, looking like his mother. It has me turning away. He's the only good thing that woman ever did but it still disturbs me when he looks like her.

"Can you get Pest for me?" He takes a pan off the stove top and dips a large spoon into it. "She's outside still."

Of course he'd ask me.

As I turn away he adds, "Be nice, Dad, she's had a long day at work."

"If she can't handle one day of work without complaining..."

"Dad!"

I raise a hand and pad barefoot to the doors, slipping on my flip-flops that sit by them.

When I exit, stepping over the puddles on the white tiles that lead from the pool, I find her standing at the stone wall, looking vacantly over the view. Peaking land, covered in green and brown can be seen to the left, straight ahead is the small town at the base of our hill, the few stores that Eastern Malibu has.

You can hear the ocean from here, smell it on the air.

The sun is setting, casting a warm glow of oranges, reds, grays, and blues in the sky. It's as though the atmosphere is on fire. It makes her bare flesh look like shimmering gold.

"Dinner is served," I say, following the soft curve of her back to her round, toned rear that would spill out of my large hands if grabbed.

She's either ignoring me or she doesn't hear me.

I refuse to call her Pest. That's my son's odd nickname for her, though I find myself at a loss for her actual name. I haven't been told it yet, likely because I haven't asked. I really should read those emails.

I click my fingers by her ear and she jolts, her faraway eyes suddenly zone back in.

"Your dinner is ready," I state.

"Oh." She smiles warmly and tucks her escaping hair behind her ear. "Thank you, Sarge."

"It's Sargent."

"Sorry. I keep doing that."

"I'm aware. I really hate it."

She grins tiredly. "I know." Little Minx. "I'm actually glad you're here. What do you want from me in return for my stay?"

"Sorry?" I stiffen, and not just my cock, at her words.

"Money, dollars, coins, etcetera." She smirks, making her red lips crinkle at the corners in a way I can't ignore. "I don't expect to stay here for free."

Tempest

"I don't need your money," he replies and turns away from me without going further into detail. "Dinner is ready."

"So what can I do instead? You have a cleaner so I can hardly help there, you have a pool boy." I follow him, careful not to slip on the tiles. "Does somebody iron for you? I could iron?"

"We'll think of something," he replies flippantly and me, being the dirty-minded woman that I am, reads into that in so many ways I shouldn't. "For now, just settle in and keep your things together, in your room and your own bathroom."

That is something I can definitely do.

He isn't done. "I hate clutter, especially that of a woman's. Just keep it all in your room."

"You got it." I inhale deeply and step inside after Sarge. "Smells great."

Maddox grins at me. I set the table, resting the placemats on the black glass surface as Sargent makes the drinks.

Sargent, such a funny name but surprisingly sexy. I feel like I'm in the army. So many unrealized fantasies are coming to mind.

"Hey, Dad," Maddox says as he brings two of the plates over.

I take my seat without thinking about it, not realizing how close my seat is to the end of the table where a certain man will be sitting. I feel my face heat with anxiety and just general shyness. I'm not typically shy but when sitting beside an attractive man who clearly hates me, it can be awkward.

I sip the white wine that has been poured for me and wonder if the bottle it came from cost more than I earned in ten hours today.

"What time do you start work tomorrow?" Maddox asks.

I cringe as I reply, "Five thirty. They want to show me how to open."

"I'll drive you," Maddox offers but I shake my head, not wanting to further burden him.

"It's not even a forty-minute walk."

"Then I'll walk you." He smiles, winking at me. "If I give you a ride, you'll get an extra hour in bed."

"When you put it that way."

"You're not insured," Sargent cuts in and Maddox winces, likely because he knows that's the truth.

"It's fine, I'll be fine..."

"I'll take you," he interrupts.

"Really." I look at the man to my left, catching his blue eyes that could freeze the earth. "I'll be fine."

"Be ready at five," he responds, and Maddox looks so happy I can't even try to say no now.

"Thank you, Mr. Wolf," I mumble, casting my eyes down on my plate.

"Are you working Monday?" Maddox asks, tapping my knee with his foot under the table.

I shrug. "I have no idea. I'm just going to say yes to whatever they offer so it's a possibility."

"Work hard and they'll never stop offering," Sargent puts in, sipping his drink softly. The way his throat bobs... why is that so appealing?

Maddox nods his agreement. "She'll have no problems there, never known somebody to not have any quit in them. Pest can go for hours."

I close my eyes and bring my fingers to the bridge of my nose. I can't believe he just said that.

"I meant while working. Not... I mean..."

"Son," Sargent warns. "Perhaps saying nothing would be prudent at this juncture."

"Right," Maddox whispers and starts laughing, quietly at first while I gulp my wine, then louder and it has me choking on the sweet fluid in my throat.

Soon we're both laughing so hard I have tears streaming down my face.

"You're such an idiot." I kick him under the table and he kicks me back, making me yelp.

We finally sober but not before I kick him again, unfortunately, as I'm pulling back my foot, it grazes across Sargent's shin and we both startle.

"Sorry," I say quietly but he doesn't reply, just finishes his dinner while Maddox and I have our banter and regale him with tales of our travels.

Tempest

Morning comes and I leave my room in my blue and white striped dress, knee-high white socks, black shoes, and white, frilly apron. I look a bit like Alice from Wonderland except my hair is darker. It's a little bit tight on my waist but otherwise fits me comfortably.

After brushing my teeth and drinking a glass of water, I skip into the hall where Sargent is already waiting for me. His hair is messy where it's usually neat, his shirt is buttoned wrong and his jeans are yesterday's.

"I almost overslept," he explains in the dark of the hall. Only the light from the moon filters in through the windows either side of the heavy front door. "Come on, let's get you to work."

I approach him, tightening my bobble as I go. "I really appreciate this."

"For my son's sake, I'm making an effort."

But not for mine, I think, but don't say. "Walking isn't a bother."

"It's too late for you to walk now," he determines, checking his phone.

He nods for me to follow him, I do, straight to the first large, metal, white door of the garage that is hiding a fucking LAMBORGHINI!

"Can I drive?" I beg, approaching the car and just staring at it. For the first time, Sargent smiles at me and it is so fucking attractive. It makes me want to sit on his....

CAR. On his car...

I was not thinking of sitting on or in, anything, but, his, car.

"Not a chance," he replies, still grinning.

The door opens upwards and he takes my hand, holding it steady as I lower myself into the vehicle. My knees are nearly higher than my lap.

"I just need to hear her purr so badly," I breathe when he climbs into his own side, still smiling.

The engine starts and I have a mini orgasm.

"Hold on," he mutters, looking as excited as I feel.

"To what?"

We rip out of the garage at a speed that other cars take minutes to reach. He skillfully maneuvers the car around the winding road that leads from the long driveway down to the bottom of the hill his home is perched on, with only two, maybe three neighboring houses lower down.

I hold onto my seat, screaming with delight as he rumbles to a stop at a junction, letting a few cars pass.

"Oh, my, God." I beam at him. "Go back up and do it again."

I'm horny. A fucking car has made me horny.

"Maybe next time," he replies, pulling out and driving at a more respectable speed now.

We stay silent the rest of the journey, until we get to the diner in question, which is dark and deathly silent.

"Stay there," Sargent orders, and climbs out only to move to my side and open the door.

"Such a gentleman." I laugh to ease my nerves as I place my hand in his and let him pull me up.

He doesn't move back far enough and my body connects with his when I stand to full height. My cheeks heat, my body burns, my nipples tighten. I stop breathing. He often has that effect on me. I wonder what he looks like under his clothing, he'd make a great subject for my art project. Maybe he'll let me draw him naked?

In my haste to move away I trip over my heel and grab onto his arm to steady myself.

"Sorry," I mumble. "I lost my handing."

My handing?

"Your handing?" He lifts a dark brow as he assesses my level of sanity.

"I meant to say footing." I side-step out of the way, eager to just get out of his life for a while. "Thank you for the ride."

He doesn't reply, but he also doesn't move until I'm inside.

"Morning," I call into the dark and move to the kitchen where light spills from under the door.

"Ah, you're here early." Bill looks thrilled. "I do love an enthusiastic worker. Coffee?"

"I would love a tea."

"Tea it is."

When I look outside, the Lamborghini is purring away, its slanted, pointed lights, shining like two sexy little beacons. Oh to be rich. Though to be honest, if I had that kind of money I'd probably just keep traveling.

Sargent

I dive into the pool, letting the cool water shock my body into submission.

My cock. It hurts. I need to get laid. I need to fuck. I need to drive into a pussy. I've never been so desperate for sex before.

I can't help it, she walks around my house without a bra, normally this wouldn't bother me, normally women are just a release, just a body I use to comfort my own when I'm the one in need. I only find them attractive when the need arises. But she's taboo, I can't have her because she's my son's which makes this all the sicker.

I grasp my dick in the water, it's still hard.

FUCKING GIVE ME STRENGTH.

Sinking to the bottom, I close my eyes and hold my breath. I meditate and calm my mind until I can't breathe then I break through the surface, take a large inhale and sink to the bottom to try again.

"Dad?" Maddox's voice is distant and muffled through the water.

I open one eye and see his rippling silhouette looming over the edge of the pool and resurface again.

"Thought you were drowning, you were under there a while." He leans in the doorway looking sleepy. It's only seven in the morning. I haven't been able to sleep since I left her at that shady-looking diner. I've passed it during my commute to work in the past but I've never been inside. It's a place where truckers stop on their way out of town or in, I doubt many locals go there. "Did you get her to work safe?"

"Of course," I reply, swimming to the edge and pulling myself up, but then I remember my throbbing cock and drop back under. "She was impressed with the car." I think back to how she responded and smile slightly. She reminded me of how I was the first time I saw a flashy car worth more than I thought I'd ever see in my lifetime. Now look at me, living the dream. I didn't get here on my own though.

"Need a hand?" My son chuckles, thinking I've fallen back in accidentally.

"Just doing push-ups," I lie and do the move a few more times.

"Show-off."

I grin at him but he rolls his eyes. Looking at him, I still can't believe my boy is a man and he has a woman, and has seen the world, not all of it but more than most. I've always been proud of him for following his dreams, never one to force on him a path that didn't entice him, but I'm happy he's back, willing to take on the business with me by his side.

We'll be a force to be reckoned with.

Just as soon as his little female distraction is gone.

"I'll be out tonight, give you and the girl some privacy."

"Where are you going?"

I wink at him. "Never you mind."

"Gross." He pretends to vomit, catching my meaning straight away.

I splash water at him as he walks away and then sink back to the bottom of the pool.

My cock still hurts.

The braless little vixen and her perfect fucking body.

"Dad?" Maddox calls, forcing me to resurface again.

"Yes, Maddox?"

"How about we go get breakfast at Bill's, surprise Pest?"

I can think of nothing worse. "No."

"Dad." He raises a brow, making him look so much like me. "Don't be boring."

"You just want me to drive you there." I see straight through his plan but find myself falling for it anyway. "Fine. I could eat. Let me shower." Before he fully vanishes, I yell, "This place better be clean!"

Tempest

"Thank you, see you soon!" I wave the family out of the door and quickly clean their table, ensuring the sugar pourer, menus, and sauces are fully stocked too.

The place isn't as busy as yesterday, but it's not empty either. Mostly single men come in, big guys in their trucks and lorries that they park across the way on the gravel carpark, or businessmen looking for a quick meal before making the commute to work.

There's one thing I'll say about this area, the men are H.O.T. HOT. And not in the *warm* sense of the word. They're gorgeous. Just because they're gorgeous. They take care of their bodies, their dark skin shining, their tan skin glowing, their pale skin steadily burning. Their smiles lovely and friendly, their banter charming. They give me the most tips so long as I meet all of the social cues and my accent sends them wild.

"You've improved a lot since yesterday," Bill comments when I bring a new order to the till. This is from creepy trucker with a tatty cap by the window.

I will never wrap my head around pancakes with syrup and bacon. Together. It sounds like a pregnancy craving, not an everyday breakfast meal.

Speaking of breakfast, I was good and ordered porridge for mine with a cup of weird-tasting tea on the side.

"I usually pick things up quickly enough." I smile in return and turn to look at the door when it jingles.

I beam from ear to eat, unable to contain my excitement when Maddox strolls in with his father who is looking around the place as though it's covered in shit, not pretty gray stripy wallpaper.

"Just a second, Bill." I stroll to Maddox and hug him. "What are you doing here?"

"Came to make sure you're working hard," he replies and I guide them to a booth in my section.

I have a section today, unlike yesterday, though the girl I'm working with called Sabrina goes out for a fag break every two minutes so I'm constantly watching her section too.

Bill either doesn't notice or doesn't care. Or perhaps he's just not in the mood to battle with her about it this early in the day.

"Menus are on the table, take a look, I can't recommend anything but the porridge or burger," I admit, shrugging. "Can I get your drinks?"

"VOS water," Sargent says, and I scribble that down in my little notepad with my fluffy-topped pen.

"Chai tea latte." Maddox yanks the menu out of the holder.

"Coming right up."

I move to Bill who is eyeing our guests curiously.

"My closest friend and his father."

"That's Sargent Wolf," he breathes, looking at the man who I live with nervously. I try not to laugh again at the name but whenever I hear it I wonder if Sarge's parents were playing a cruel joke on him. He sounds like a character off Nickelodeon, not a millionaire bachelor with a successful partnership in an international business. "He's in my diner."

Is he some kind of local celebrity or anomaly? Perhaps a serial killer?

"Cap wants you by the window." Bill nods to the creepy trucker with his faded blue cap and white shirt with greasy stains down the front and yellow stains around the armpits.

I approach his table with a smile like at any other table and get my notepad ready to add to his order. My memory is good enough but the foods here are different to back home, I don't want to mess up.

"How long will my food be?" His voice is gruff and scratchy, I try not to cringe at the strong stench of stale fags coming from his dirty self.

"I'll just check on that for you."

"Yeah, you do that," he murmurs as I walk away and I vaguely hear him comment, "Sweet ass."

But I ignore it because I work for tips, not for an hourly wage.

Bill dings a bell on the counter. "Drinks, Pest."

I grab a round tray and place the drinks onto it while asking, "How long on Cap's food? He's asking."

"He ordered ten minutes ago. This isn't Burger King," he grumbles. "Tell him another ten minutes at least. Perfect pancakes like ours take time."

I nod and carry the tray carefully to Maddox and Sarge who are both still looking at their menus.

"Any idea what you want to eat?" I tuck the tray under my arm after putting their drinks before them and pull out my pad and pen.

"*Oatmeal* with blueberries and maple syrup," Maddox says and looks at his dad who tosses his menu down on the table and relaxes back in the bench seat.

"Same, minus the syrup, extra blueberries."

"Fabulous," I singsong, still smiling as I scribble. "This reminds me of when we met."

Maddox nods. "I was just thinking that."

"You were a waitress?"

"No, but I thought she was. Called her to my table in Thailand. She was wearing this black dress that was so similar to all of the other servers."

"I thought he was hitting on me and then he just looked at me and said..."

"VOS!" We both burst into laughter together.

I add when I've calmed enough to talk, "Except *he* said please."

"Funny." Sarge rolls his eyes. "And you've lived a fairy tale ever since."

"It has been pretty smooth sailing, hasn't it, Pest?"

I nod, smiling warmly at my friend. "Let me get your orders in and I'll be back."

I rush their ticket to Bill who takes it and hobbles to the kitchen, handing it to the cooks through a hole in the wall.

"Hey!" Cap yells and I cringe. I got distracted.

I race over to him, smiling nervously because he looks really pissed off.

"I'm sorry," I immediately say. "Bill tells me it'll only be a few more minutes while..."

"You gonna give me the same hug you gave that faggot when he walked in?"

Did he really just say that? Is faggot still an insult used these days? It's disgusting.

"I... I... umm..." I stammer, glancing at Maddox over my shoulder and finding his eyes on the man. I don't think he heard him call him that heinous word, but I know he heard him shout "hey" at me. "They are perfecting your pancakes as we speak."

I walk away before losing my temper and stop at another

two traveling men as I pass. They are much politer and eager to smile at me.

"You okay?" Maddox asks, his brows pulled in with a frown. I notice Sargent's eyes are on the man too. He looks livid.

"I'm fine, honestly, he's just hungry." I wink at Sargent this time and smile when he raises a thick, pointed brow. "Your porridge won't be long."

"Oatmeal," Maddox singsongs.

"Porridge," I singsong back.

"Porridge sounds tastier than oatmeal." Sargent shrugs, looking human and less annoyed for once in my presence. Also, he just agreed with me. Hell has frozen over.

"The same way pussy sounds better than vagina." Cap roars with laughter at his own joke, banging his hand on the table which startles the rest of the room, including Sabrina who has finally returned and is wiping down the clean tables in her own section to make it look like she's working.

Which means, if he can hear us then they heard him and what he said.

I sigh.

"Speaking of pussy, walk yours over here with my breakfast." He looks at Bill. "Least she's nice to look at, if not a bit slow."

"Leave it," I say to Maddox when he shifts in his seat.

Bill rings the bell so I scarper away, quickly grabbing the rude arse-wipe's breakfast and taking it to him.

"Now that's more like it." He grins, showing yellow teeth beyond his bristly, graying moustache that hangs over his top lip. "Do I get my hug now?"

"I don't know you," I reply, trying to look apologetic. "I'm not a hugger."

His lip curls with a sneer, raising his moustache to his nose. Yep. I just lost my tip.

I move to Bill and grab the drinks from the counter, getting back to work.

~

Sargent

Does this attitude work for him? Does he get laid when he speaks to and treats people badly like this? I have to say, I admire the girl's professionalism and calm. I'm on the edge of my seat and I don't even like her all that much. I respect her but I don't like her. I don't trust her. Though she doesn't deserve this.

She brings over our oatmeal and rolls her eyes when I clean my spoon with my water and a napkin.

"It's clean," she snaps but I see her lips twitch.

"Your version of clean and mine are very different," I respond, referring to the fact she dropped an orange segment on the floor the second day she was here, picked it up and ate it anyway without rinsing it.

"Are you trying to say I'm dirty?"

"Well, you're not what I would call clean by my standards."

"He's OCD, you've seen his house," Maddox replies, touching my pinkie finger gently. "He didn't mean anything by it."

"You say that about everything he says," she snaps, pulling her hand away. I watch her close her eyes and count down from four before plastering a new smile on her face.

"I didn't see popcorn on the menu, surely it should be provided when receiving a show with food?" I comment and she actually takes a step at me.

"Okay." Maddox stands and places his hand on her stomach as I smile at her in a way I know is pissing her off. I really do rub her the wrong way.

Her pretty hazel eyes glower at me but I just find her even sexier than usual. I love it that I can piss her off to the extent where she wants to rip out my hair, but dirty fucktard near the window can't even get her to drop her smile.

Does she find me attractive?

All signs point to yes. Now isn't that an interesting development?

Especially now that Maddox has declared he'll be going to England with her in six months for a while when her visa expires, which will likely turn into forever. It was a conversation we had on the way here when discussing work.

Why couldn't he have fallen for a local girl? There are so many.

Though I must admit not many quite have the same charm as his little Pest.

If any charm at all.

"Stop being a jerk," Maddox snaps and I know I might have gone a bit too far this time. I'm purposely goading her but my son keeps defending me. It'll be their downfall.

Here's hoping.

"I wasn't," I lie, using my most innocent mask.

He doesn't look as though he's falling for it.

Moments pass before the man by the window shouts, "HEY!" like before. My hands clench on the table, on either side of my nearly empty bowl. The oatmeal isn't as bad as I thought it would be and the blueberries were fresh and clean.

She takes his bill to him, without even asking and waits for him to cash out. He's whispering something to her but I can't quite make out what he's saying. The twitching of her fingers tells me she's really struggling to stay calm now.

I'm ready to go over there myself when she finally turns with his money in hand and he whistles loudly, stands and grabs a handful of her ass.

"Fucking nice," he chuckles.

My eyes cloud over with red and I stand from my seat, so does Maddox, but before either of us take a step she's turning on him.

Her fingers grab his nose and she twists. There's an audible pop, a gruff cry of pain, and then, when she plants her knee in his groin, he goes down. One hand to his nose, the other to his limp dick.

The Pest has some fight in her.

"Ah shit," she mutters and brings her notepad to her face.

Tempest

F ucking fuming is an understatement.

I got fired. FIRED. For laying that shit for brains out.

It was my second day. That has got to be a new record. I should sue him and shut that place down.

"I'm never eating there again!" I yell, punching the bag hanging from the ceiling. It's heavy so it doesn't sway. I bring my foot around and kick it and hit it with three more jabs. "I'm never even walking past there again!" I spin and kick but it's clumsy and I fall onto my side.

Hopping back up using my shoulders, I launch some more controlled jabs on the bag.

"Who do they think they are? He grabbed my arse!"

So, screaming at a punching bag, alone, in a gym in the room behind the garage isn't probably the best way to announce my *sanity* to the world. But it is how I cope. It's how I deal. This, meditation, and a lot of breathing are how I stay in control of myself.

I don't lose control, ever.

I didn't lose control in the diner either.

"He deserved it, damn it!"

"I agree."

I tense and stop hopping from foot to foot. A bead of sweat trails from my neck, down my spine. It's wet but it does nothing to douse the fire I feel inside.

"I'm not in the mood," I snap, pressing a wrapped hand to the smooth, cool surface of the bag. "Please. Just, not now, Sarge."

"Mr. Wolf."

"I'm not calling you Mr. Wolf. You sound like a fucking nursery rhyme," I mutter, knowing he can hear me and not caring because I'm already really bloody angry and there's no way I can feel worse than I do already.

I move to the window and stretch, not turning once to look at him, though I can vaguely see his reflection in the window if I focus on it enough.

"Stay right where you are," he orders, exiting the room. "Do not move a muscle."

I don't know why I listen. My sweat-drenched body, in my old leggings and older sports bra, is starting to get chilly. My breathing is finally steadying, and I can feel that peace coming on that exercise brings.

His footsteps come back and I hear a click that has me tensing.

Is he taking my picture?

"Don't move," he warns.

It is so hard to stay still when somebody has told you to.

"Stay right there." His voice is a whisper as he gets closer, looking for the perfect angle through the lens as the setting sun glows a fiery orange around us. I feel its heat through the glass and subconsciously reach out to touch it. When I realize what I've done I cringe, waiting for him to snap or shout but he simply takes a few steps back and I hear the clicking of the shutter again.

"Jesus," he murmurs so quietly I'm not sure that's what he actually said. And if it is what he said, I have no idea what it means, I just know the intensity of it gave me a little clenching tingle in my womb.

With my hand flat on the glass and my fingers splayed, I close my eyes and try to keep still like he said.

I'm waiting for him to start laughing and say that this is a prank but how can it be when there's such a raw and powerful energy charging in the air between us?

I swallow and my head drops forward slightly, as it does, I hear his footsteps move back toward the door.

He says gruffly, his tone deep and quiet, "As you were."

And that's that.

I relax and sit on the floor, taking in the sight of the sun sinking into the horizon. It's such a peaceful view.

Sargent

"There's a party on the beach tonight, my old friends are going," Maddox tells me when his *Pest* leaves us alone to watch TV on the second floor.

She's doing what she can to avoid me, I've likely confused her or upset her. Though I have noticed how she hasn't told Maddox about my capturing her image.

How could I resist?

She was sweating, shimmering, glowing, her toned back and legs just caught the light in such a way. I wanted to rub oil all over her body, taking my time at each dip and curve.

I need to stop thinking about it.

I contemplate telling Maddox but for some reason I can't, which is how I know whatever happened in that gym was less than innocent artistry. She knows it too or she herself would have approached the subject with my son.

I've confused her. I've confused myself.

I rub my face with my hands.

"Dad, you listening?"

I nod once.

"So we won't be home until late, if at all." He taps away on his phone screen.

"Let me guess, you need a ride?"

"Can't you just insure me?"

I smirk and ask, "I thought you wanted to do this on your own?"

"You can take it out of my first paycheck."

At that I laugh. "We'll see what we can do."

We share a smile before he continues, "As for a ride, Kirk's coming to get us."

Ugh, Kirk. I like the guy but he smokes too much weed.

"Well, you kids have fun, don't go swimming if you're

drinking and please stay out of trouble. At your age you can't get away with playing the teen angst card."

"We'll take you with us and play the AARP card instead."

"Little shit," I murmur, smiling at his audacity. I am not old. People often think we're brothers, not father and son. He doesn't know what he's talking about.

I am far more offended by this than I should be.

"Come on, Pest!" Maddox yells from the door.

I watch her come skidding out of her room in flip-flops, denim shorts, a bikini top, and a patterned white tank top that's so translucent it may as well not exist. Her thick, dark brown hair is in two braids and she has a pair of sunglasses resting on her hairline.

"See you later, Mr. Wolf." She grins, waving as she passes.

I get the scent of vanilla and spices I can't name as she flutters past, her flip-flops clapping against the ground as she goes.

They race to his friend's sports car and I do the fatherly thing and yell, "SEATBELTS!"

Maddox just gives me a look. I know it's ridiculous, he's been traveling through countries unknown for some time, but I still worry.

Sighing as they speed away while cheering loudly, I close the door and return to my empty home.

Then I call my own friends and invite them over because fuck this silence.

My phone is ringing. Why is it ringing?

It's one in the morning, I've been asleep for maybe forty minutes.

I remember Maddox went out and panic holds my heart in a tight fist.

"Dad?" There's the sound of a loud beat in the background and people laughing and talking. At least if people are laughing and talking that means nothing bad has happened. Or so I deduce.

"What's wrong?" I ask immediately, sitting up and reaching for the lamp.

"Nothing, just, Pest is on her way home, she's drunk. Can you make sure she gets home okay and text me when she does? She'll pass out and forget."

My panic leaves me, and in its place comes anger. "Why haven't you escorted her home yourself?"

"Because I don't want to go yet and... well... you know. Pest is cool with it. She's in an Uber."

"You abandoned your girl to a fucking Uber?" Did I just step into an alternate reality? I know I'm not the cheeriest, nicest guy to be around, but I'd never abandon my date to a fucking taxi alone. "And she's *cool* with that?"

"Why wouldn't she be?" He chuckles and I hear a female in the background shouting for him to hurry up. "Just make sure she gets in safely."

What kind of man did I raise?

I blow out a breath and climb out of bed, flipping the thin blanket back as I go. I don a black T-shirt with some kind of logo on the front and make my way downstairs. My room is the only room upstairs, the rest of the upstairs is an office and second den. Or it is now that she's here. It mostly went unused until her.

I wait for what feels like hours before I see headlights in the driveway. It has only been fifteen minutes, if that.

"Thank you!" I hear her call after a car door slams and as her feet carry her closer, I open the door.

She staggers right into my chest with an oomph and a very inebriated giggle.

I try not to think of her heat, or how perfectly she'd fit in my arms were I to wrap them around her. I definitely try not to think of the latter.

"Oops." With her hand on my chest and the other clutching her flip-flops, she beams at me in the dark. Her smile is lopsided but strangely adorable. "Sorry, Mr. Wolf." And then she wobbles past.

I watch as she hops on one foot and yanks on her ankle.

"What are you doing?"

"Duh," she replies deeply and grins at me as she hops. "Trying to take off my shoe."

She starts to fall to the side so I grab her elbow to steady her. "You're not wearing any shoes."

Her foot hits the floor and she wriggles her painted toes on the wooden floor. When her wide eyes come back up to mine, her lips pinch together and she bursts into a fit of giggles so strong I laugh with her. Though only a little.

I don't want her to think I find her cute, endearing, and funny because I do not.

"I'm so high," she giggles, shaking her head. Her eyes become round with panic. "On life, Mr. Wolf. Not weed. Life."

I pretend to not hear her or see her drop her flip-flops onto the floor.

"Mr. Wolf?" She dips her head to catch my eyes with hers. Hers are round, innocent, wild, glowing, alert, but also drunk, definitely high, and tired.

"Yes?"

"Are you gay?"

I absolutely love freedom of life and love but having such an attractive woman think I'm gay raises my hackles.

"I am not."

"Because it's cool if you are," she mumbles, lifting the see-through tank top over her head as I guide her to her bedroom. "No judgment. Love and be loved. It would just shine a light on why you hate women."

I clench my jaw. "I'm not gay and I don't hate women. I just don't like to live with a woman."

"But I'm such a ray of sunshine," she giggles, throwing her arms out so suddenly her hand connects with my cheek.

Growling, I grab her wrist as she laughs even harder and cups my face with her hand.

"I'm sorry, Sarge, I didn't see you there."

I ignore her and push open her bedroom door, but she suddenly stops and places her hands against the frame. "Shall we order pizza?"

"No, it's one in the morning."

"Oh." Her bottom lip sticks out when I grab her arm and force her into her room. "Can I draw you?"

"Why are you so random?" I murmur, pushing her away from me when she places her hand on my chest again. She needs to stop touching me, my cock is finally behaving, but not if she keeps touching me.

"Can I? You took my picture, it's only fair."

I open my mouth to speak but my jaw hangs when she suddenly drops her denim shorts and steps out of them. She's wearing a thong. A black, lace thong that sits on the curves of her ass perfectly.

My cock definitely isn't behaving now. Shit. It hurts. It's straining against my boxers and if she turns around now, she'll see it, but I can't move. I can't look away.

"You're not answering which means that's a yes." She grins over her shoulder as she unhooks the back of her bikini top and lifts the neck loop over her head.

I finally turn around, finding the strength and common sense to do so.

This is my son's girl and she's undressing in front of his father. She's everything I thought she was and worse.

I should just fuck her and show him what a little cunt she really is, but I don't want to be the cause of his hurt.

"You're disgusting," I snarl at her without looking behind me. "Have some self-respect."

As I leave I don't look back, not even when she throws something at the door right by my head.

If I disliked her before, I hate her now.

Sargent

The second Maddox walks in at five in the morning, I stop him in the hall.

"Don't leave me to babysit her again, do you understand?" I snarl and he's so startled he backs up a step.

"What the fuck, Dad?" He frowns, his happy drunken smile gone. "What happened?"

I run a hand through my hair. Do I tell him? He should know.

"She got naked," I blurt and my voice sounds higher than it should. "I helped her to her bedroom and she got naked."

He just stares at me for the longest time, blinking slowly before his lips twitch. "I mean, yeah, I should have warned you. She does that when she's high."

"Does what?"

"She calls it becoming one with nature." He chuckles as though it's not a big deal. Am I making it a big deal?

"She got naked in front of your father."

"She's not underage, Dad, chill, and she doesn't have the worst body in the world to look at. Why are you so upset?"

How can he be so flippant and easy about all of this? If she were mine I'd be raging. But then again, I always have had a temper and been possessive.

"You've got to get your kicks somewhere," he adds, laughing harder.

Little twerp. I get plenty of kicks.

I follow him into the kitchen where he moves to the fridge.

"Is that all she did? That's why you're mad? Because she stripped in a room she's staying in?" He takes a swig of juice and waits for my answer.

"I'm going to bed," I say and skulk to my room. "Keep her out of my way."

"Dad," he shouts after me but I ignore him.

What the hell kind of man have I raised?

Tempest

When I wake up the next morning, in bed, nude from head to toe, blankets kicked onto the floor, I groan and roll onto my back, scratching at the tattoo on my arm.

"Morning, sleepy." Maddox grins from the doorway, tossing me one of his oversized shirts.

"Morning," I reply and pull it on before sitting up on the side of my bed. "My head is spinning."

"Mine too," he admits, chuckling. "But you might want to

avoid my dad today, you gave his aging heart a bit too much excitement last night."

"Oh, I know," I reply bitterly, my bad mood increasing. "He called me disgusting. That's something I won't be forgetting any time soon."

"He what?" Maddox's smile vanishes.

"I wasn't thinking, okay? I just started getting undressed and he was there. He didn't see anything anyway; my back was to him," I ramble and then move my tongue around my mouth. I taste like sand and feet. I need to brush my teeth.

I pad into the en suite.

He follows. "What did he say?"

"Just that: *you're disgusting.*" I shrug like his words didn't hurt but they did. "He's so harsh. Like I was *steaming,* mate. I wasn't thinking about his sensitive little eyes. I'm not that hideous, am I?"

"No," Maddox assures me. "I'd fuck you if I didn't consider you family now."

"Not a visual I want, Maddox." I giggle at him and start vigorously cleaning my teeth. "I'll be out soon anyway, I need to look for a new job, or beg for my old one back."

"I'll have a word with my dad."

"No!" I blurt, dribbling foamy toothpaste down my chin. "Please, don't. It'll make things awkward."

"He needs to chillax."

"I know, but he won't if you start on at him." I splash water on my face and turn to him. He hands me a towel, I thank him and dab my cheeks and nose gently. "Let me deal with this myself, okay?"

"Fine, but if he gets too much for you just tell me and I'll sort him out."

My arms wrap around his waist as I drop the towel onto the ground and we hug in the middle of the bathroom.

"What time is it?" I ask quietly, inhaling his scent. He's showered already, I can smell his peppery shower gel and a spritz of aftershave.

"Noon."

"Shit," I murmur and release him. "And where's your dad so I can avoid him?"

"In his office probably."

He's not in his office, I discover when I creep into the kitchen for food, wearing a white vest and the same shorts I wore last night. They're clean enough and the rest of my clothes are in the dryer. I chucked them in last night before I went out.

I don't greet him as he eats a slice of toast and reads a newspaper. I do however look at him and narrow my eyes when his come to mine.

"Morning," he tries but I turn away from him and grab a yogurt from the fridge.

Just as I pull myself up onto the counter, mostly because I know he hates it, a man walks in from outside. I didn't spot him before but I do now and my lips part.

He's delicious, muscular, with dark skin and hazel eyes. He's tall too, nearly as tall as Sargent and Maddox but not quite.

When he sees me, he crosses the distance, wearing a light gray vest that covers nothing and white board shorts that cover too much.

"You must be *the girl*, it's a pleasure. I'm Devon but everybody calls me Dev." His smile is as charming as his tone. "I don't think I can recall your name though?"

I notice how he said, *the girl*. Likely because that's what Sargent always calls me. God forbid he should actually be polite. It's nice that he has polite friends at least.

"Tempest." I place my hand into his and try not to blush. "It's nice to meet you."

"Your name is Tempest?" Sargent asks, looking between me and his friend. Or I assume they're friends, they look to be around the same age. I can see him trying to fight a smile.

"You have a problem with my name now too?" I snap, hating that he has the power to irritate me so easily.

"I think it's a beautiful name." Devon catches my eyes and his easy smile makes my frown melt away. "Are you named after the play or the storm?"

"I don't know," I admit, shrugging.

His smile remains in place. "Have you ever seen the play?"

"Unfortunately, no, but it's on my bucket list."

"Oh yeah? What else is on your bucket list?" he asks, sounding genuinely interested. Before I can reply though, he flips the conversation. "So, let me just get my ducks in a row here... You're Maddox's girlfriend, right?"

I laugh at that. "No. Definitely not."

"So, you're single?"

"Devon," Sargent snarls and Devon raises his hands defensively.

"I'm just scooping the gossip." He chuckles moving away and sitting on a stool a few down from Sargent who is glaring at me. "I must have misheard. This asshole told me you were his son's girl?"

I shake my head. "No, Mad and I have never been like that. We were always just friends and hopefully always will be."

His thick, black brows almost hit his hairline of tight, black curls. "Well isn't that an interesting development?"

"What is?" Maddox finally joins me, getting his own yogurt from the fridge and spoon from the drawer by my thigh.

"He thinks we're together," I say, pointing at Devon with my thumb.

Maddox rolls his eyes. "Who doesn't when they first meet us? Just ask Dad, we sleep in separate beds and everything."

"In that case, are you free tonight?" Devon asks good-naturedly.

"Fuck off, Dev, you're like twice her age," Maddox laughs, pulling himself up onto the counter beside me.

"Behave yourself, Dev," Sargent warns but Devon seems to think they're both hilarious. "Are you joining us outside, Maddox?"

"No, I've got that fucking freight to oversee at the docks, remember?"

Sargent nods. "I'd almost forgotten. You sure you can handle it?"

"It's just inventory before sailing." Maddox hops down and tosses his empty yogurt pot into the recycling bin. "I'll be fine. I'll call you if I need anything."

Dev looks at me and asks, "Are you joining us today?"

"I'm going job hunting." I look at Maddox who winks at me. "He's dropping me in town on his way to work."

"I'd be glad to escort you," Devon tries again, looking at Sargent and grinning when he glares at him.

"It'll be boring," I laugh nervously, hoping they don't make me put them out. "I'm just handing in my CV to anywhere that will take it."

Sargent

I watch one of my oldest friends flirt unabashedly with the girl who I now know to be called, Tempest. Even going as far as to offer her a job at his surfing business doing admin work.

Oh he wants to fuck her and he isn't ashamed to show it. He's always been a dog and until now it never bothered me.

"Well then it's settled, you'll start Monday, I'll even throw in some surfing lessons."

"She can already surf," Maddox states. "She's pretty good actually. We learned in Thailand."

"It was incredible," she adds and the way she breathes the words has my cock twitching again. I wonder if she'll say that exact statement about me when I finish inside of her, buried deep in her tight little... Well, my thoughts just went elsewhere that's for sure. "But I can't just accept a job."

"Sure you can, Maddox is family and you're his guest, which means we've got to take care of you too," Devon replies, suave and easy.

I've never hated him until the moment she blushes and

starts giggling. It's definitely hate I feel toward him now. Complete loathing.

"Excuse me while I vomit." I stand and leave the room, unable to watch this anymore.

I'm still trying to wrap my head around the fact Maddox and she aren't together. I don't recall a single time they've kissed or really touched in a way that could be deemed romantic. I've never seen them go to bed together. It seems so obvious now, especially with how he reacted in the early hours to the fact she got naked in my presence.

Why didn't I read the fucking emails?

That still doesn't mean he's not going to fall in love with her and leave me forever, alone in this place. I'd have to follow him across the globe just to see my grandkids grow up.

I'm not old enough to be thinking of grandkids yet but with us having only my ex-wife's mother and father left over in LA, family is important to me. My son is important to me. He's all I have really. His family is my future.

Now that I don't have a relationship to break up, I know there's going to be no convincing him to stay.

Suddenly it's not about destroying what they have, now it's about convincing *her* to stay behind. If she falls in love with it here, will my son stay where she is? The only reason he planned to go to England is because of her. Isn't it?

I've been tackling this from the wrong angle. I'm supposed to be smarter than this.

"Dad?" Maddox snaps, coming after me.

I stop in the hall and watch his blue eyes blaze with fury.

"Yes, Son?"

"Lay off," he snaps. "Stop being a dick, stop speaking to her like shit. Lay off her or we're leaving, I'm not kidding."

Yep. I've definitely been doing this all wrong.

"Why do you hate her so much? What has she done to you? She's followed your rules, she has been respectful and kind..."

"I'll make more of an effort," I reply softly, taking him off guard. "I've been a dick, but I'll extend an olive branch. Happy?"

"Yes," he grunts, crossing his arms over his chest. "Thank you." Then he adds, "And don't let Devon touch her, she's not like him, she puts her fucking heart into everything and if he hurts her, it'll cause problems between me and him. Okay? Watch him with her."

Well... shit. "Fine. Anything else?"

"Promise me you'll keep an eye on her today."

"I promise." I mean it too. There's not a chance in hell I'm letting them do anything. He's twice her age. It's wrong.

So why is it whenever I close my eyes at night it's all I can think about, her riding my cock, scratching her nails across my chest...

I'm hard again.

Fuck. I really need to get laid.

Maddox rushes to his room to get changed for work and I rush to mine to wait for my dick to sit the hell down and shut up.

When I return to the kitchen it's empty, so I follow the sounds of Devon and her voices to outside where they're both stretching out on the sun loungers surrounding the firepit by the windows to the gym.

Devon is trying to pretend he isn't watching her as she rubs lotion on her legs and feet. I have to think about old lady vaginas to stop myself from getting hard again. Especially when she straddles the fabric lounger and rubs the white, creamy substance into her chest. She's wearing shorts but I can see the apex of her thighs beyond the denim. All she'd have to do is shift the wrong way...

Devon looks at me and then thanks the heavens with his hands under his chin. She doesn't notice.

I see him getting more and more excited when it comes to doing her back, he's going to offer; normally she gets Maddox to do it for her and I remember wondering how he did it without pinning her down and fucking her where she lay at the time. Then I also remember thinking how he's probably getting bored of her having been with her for a year already.

Now, I'm going to have to figure that out for myself because I'm snatching the bottle from her hand and yanking her hair roughly to the side. She has no clue how much I want to wrap this braid around my hand and use it as leverage for when I pound her from behind.

"What are you doing?" She doesn't sound pleased and yips when I pour the cold lotion onto her shoulders.

"Maddox isn't here," I reply, my tone coming out tense as usual. I just don't know how to relax around her. Especially now that my fingers are finally touching her skin.

I move both of my hands over her shoulders and she slowly releases the tension in them.

Old wrinkly vagina lips. Dog sperm. Dying whales. Moldy bread and cheese.

I rotate through a list of disgusting things as her smooth back quivers under my touch.

My fingers drag the lotion to her waist and my palms massage it in. I have to sit sideways as I'm doing it for fear of losing control and pulling her back into my groin.

It would be so easy to lay her down, remove her shorts, and push into her. I bet she'd be so tight and warm, wet and willing. Her raspy, sexy-as-sin voice will whimper in my ear as I bury my cock all the way to the hilt.

"I'm sorry about what I said last night," I say quietly, to change the subject, as I rub the last of the lotion in and try not to cry at the fact I don't have an excuse to touch her anymore. "I'm a jerk. I've never been a very kind person as it is but I'm going to try and be better."

She turns to look at me and places her sticky-from-the-lotion hand onto mine, which is the same. "So, a fresh start?"

"A fresh start," I agree, wetting my lip when her minty, fruity breath fans against them.

"Does that mean I can draw you?"

I wasn't expecting that.

"My profile?" I can't say no to that.

"No," she smiles and lowers her voice, "I draw nude models."

My breath catches in my throat and Devon sits up and looks at me having heard what she just asked. Has she forgotten he's still here?

"For artistic purposes," she defends, grinning. "It wouldn't be like, *weird*, I'm professional. I'm not trying to get you naked for other reasons."

That's disappointing.

"I need a drink," Devon laughs and she joins in, looking embarrassed for a moment as he passes and offers us both one.

"Let me show you my portfolio first." She squeezes my hand. "Before you make a decision."

"Why do you want to draw me nude? Why can't I be clothed?"

"Because I'm working on a series that I've named, *The Divine Skin.*"

Fuck me. I just... this girl... "Fine, but only if you allow me to photograph you in return."

She looks as startled as I felt when she asked. I'm bluffing of course, I mean, I wouldn't mind it but I'm hoping she'll say no so I can too.

So quickly I add, "First."

"For artistic purposes?"

Holy fuck she's actually considering it!

I nod, my mouth is dry, my tongue thick.

"Okay, deal." She removes her hand and holds out her other one to shake. "Though I don't know why you want to photograph me..."

"I could say the same for you wanting to draw me."

"You're kidding right? You're like Zeus except younger, darker, and more attractive! Your body is what society would deem the *perfect* male body."

"Maddox..." I say stupidly, yet my ego is taking in all the air it can, swelling and tripling in size at her words. A woman half my age thinks I'm perfect.

"I've already drawn Maddox. I've seen him naked more times than I've seen him clothed."

She really is looking at this from a purely innocent and artistic angle. Still, it's nice to know she thinks I have a great body. I wonder what she'll think of my cock.

I also wonder what she'll look like completely naked in the setting sun. There's something about the way the sun shines on her skin, its color and little dips and grooves. It's like crack to me. I need to see it again. Which reminds me that the photographs I took before need to be developed, I've been putting it off. I might never stop looking at them and now that I know she's not with my son and never has been, I'll feel less guilty about it.

Tempest

When Devon leaves a few hours later, having calmed down significantly, I find myself feeling almost nervous.

I'm on the lounger, comfortable, a drink in hand when I sit up and look at Sargent across the way. He's reading a novel that's casting a shade onto his groin area. Not that I'm looking.

I have to be professional, this is all purely for artistic purposes.

So why is the thought of him naked, his cock sticking up ramrod straight, making me wetter than the fucking pool beside us?

"Sarge?"

He lowers his book and gazes at me. His eyes and demeanor toward me have softened significantly today. He's been kind, asking me questions, and genuinely wanting to know the answers. Especially about my travels.

I showed them both my drawings too and they were very impressed. It made me feel good.

I wonder what he'll think of my paintings.

At one point he even said that I'm a lot smarter than he originally thought. I wasn't sure if that was an insult or not but I smiled and nodded anyway.

"Yes, Tempest?" That's the first time he's said my name since he discovered it and it sends a thrill through my body that has me shaking with desire.

I am fucked. Or I want to be.

By Maddox's father or just in general? Shit.

Maddox will have a fit.

"Shall we do the art things?"

"Art things?" He too sits up and raises a thick brow. "You want to do it now?"

Yes, I want to do it now. "I just really want to draw you as soon as possible." I am being professional. I am. This isn't about seeing him naked. Or it wasn't. I don't even like him but I can appreciate an attractive body when I see one.

He blows out a breath and shifts in his seat. "Sure. Why don't you go and shower off the suntan lotion and meet me in my room when you're done?"

I nod nervously and stand.

He watches me go a few steps before asking, "You sure about this? You can back out."

"It's all for the art," I reply quietly and wave at him over my shoulder.

～

Sargent

I'm nervous. This is happening. I don't know how it began happening but it's happening. Though she could still back out.

I've never wanted to take a photograph more in my entire life.

This is groundbreaking for me. This feeling, it's taking me back to my younger years when photography was all I could think about.

I check the tripods are functional for the fifth time and turn on my digital camera. I have one antique camera that I use and one very expensive digital camera. I like the way they both capture images. The digital is clear and crisp whereas the antique puts a natural sepia over everything.

There's not a software in the world that can perfectly mimic an old camera like mine. It would have been state of the art once upon a time and is likely worth a fair bit these days.

There's a gentle knock on the door. I move to it, my camera hanging around my neck.

I'm relieved to see she has washed and dried her hair, it's floating in thick curtains of dark brown around her shoulders. There's no makeup on her face and there's nothing but a fluffy towel around her body which she's holding onto for dear life.

This is insane. I can't believe we're doing this.

She takes in the setup, the thick, cream fur rug on the ground by the window which has an even better view of Malibu than the garden.

"Don't be nervous," I assure her, unsure on how to approach her.

"I'm not," she lies and gulps audibly. "Where do you want me?"

Over my bed, on the floor, on all fours, on my face.

"On... On the rug, just there." I point and move the tripod out of the way.

I turn away when she starts to unwrap the towel. I hear it drop on the floor and bite hard on my lip.

"Shall I lie down?"

"Please," I reply and inhale a deep breath before looking at her.

She sits on her side first, her legs bent as she takes in the view, her back to me as the sun finally starts to set.

"Wait," I bark when she starts to move. I take a couple of shots of her just like that. I never take so many shots. I line up the perfect ones and click. There's something about her that has me wanting to capture every single angle of her physical soul. "Okay, lie down."

I push my fist into my mouth to stop myself from groaning when I see it all. All of her beautiful body, every naked inch of flesh that I so badly wanted to see last night but couldn't allow myself the pleasure.

Her round breasts are soft against her chest which rises and falls slowly. Her bare mound is slightly hidden by her leg which is raised higher than the other, a subconscious way of offering herself a little modesty.

I want to part her thighs and slot myself between them.

I stand on the stepladder to get a bit of height over her but it's not right. The lighting isn't catching her body the way it did before. The picture isn't perfect, not that her body isn't perfect. I've never seen a nicer body. I've never craved a nicer body.

"I'll be just a moment," I whisper softly and she bites her lip much like I just did. Her eyes don't meet mine.

I grab what I need and race back to her, praying she hasn't moved, praying the sunset hasn't suddenly vanished. It's a ridiculous thought but one I can't help. I have just a short amount of time to get this right.

"Take your time," she mumbles playfully and then grins at me. Her face is so beautiful, her soft features and tilted wide eyes, her near symmetrical face, her hazel-green eyes. All of it the perfect combination.

"Sorry." I raise the bottle of body oil and bag of ice

"What are you doing?" She doesn't look happy to see the props.

"It's for the shot," I reply but I'm not so sure it is. "It smells like strawberries." Tastes like it too but I leave that part out.

I squirt the oil on her chest and midriff and she murmurs a breathy, "Oh my God."

"Do you want to do the honors?"

"Duh." She rubs it in herself and it's even more erotic than watching her with the suntan lotion. "This is just so fucking random." I smile at her and her eyes scan my face. "Promise me you won't post these all over the internet."

"On my honor," I reply, taking an ice cube out of the bag when she lies back down. I don't ask her permission this time, because I'm not thinking. Because I'm an idiot. A crafty, clever idiot.

I roll the ice cube over her left nipple where the tiny silver balls of her piercing peek out of the sides. The ice cube catches it gently and I have to fight the urge to tease it with my tongue.

She gasps at the contact and swallows before blowing out a breath between her parted lips.

I'm getting hard again.

She watches me as I lose myself, totally transfixed by the way her nipple tightens and extends.

I lower my head and hear her breath catch in her throat when I start to blow on her, to dry the water that's rolling down the oily sheen that really does smell like strawberries. The oil was a gift that I got in a bag from an event I attended last year. I thought it was stupid but it really has come in handy.

When I move the ice cube to her other nipple she grabs my wrist and squirms while saying, "This is starting to feel less artistic and more like foreplay."

She said foreplay.

I snap back into the now.

I quickly stand, climb the small ladder and take the shots with both of my cameras.

She moves her body how I ask, just little adjustments here and there as I get the perfect images. It's better than expected. Her pebbled nipples, her wide eyes holding arousal, her lips swollen and parted as though waiting for a kiss. Her incredible, bare pussy that I want to touch.

I get plenty of incredible shots but I want more, so many more and there's just one part of her that she's missed.

I take the oil again as she fans out her hair and squeeze it onto the part of thigh that doesn't hold the same sheen the rest of her body does.

She jolts and frowns at me. "What are you doing?"

"The sun's about to set, we missed a spot." I don't wait for permission, I place my hand on her thigh and rub.

A gasped breath releases from between her parted lips as she watches what I'm doing.

~

Tempest

His hand gently massages the oil in, even after the spot I missed is covered. He's in a trance like before when he was teasing my nipples.

I'm aroused and his hand is not helping.

He's getting higher and higher, completely abandoning his camera to use his other hand to lean on as he strokes my inner thigh.

When his finger gets so close I can feel the heat of it against my rapidly moistening sex, my eyes flutter closed and I moan. I try to stop myself but it's too intense. There's too much of every-thing happening. I want him to touch me. More than I've ever wanted to be touched.

Then his hand goes back down, past my knee. I feel almost disappointed until it starts coming back up again.

He doesn't try to make eye contact, I'm glad. I'm in a happy little bubble right now. My body is responding in ways it never has for anyone.

"Jesus," he whispers when he finally makes contact and slips his finger into the wetness between my thighs. I whimper, shifting on the soft rug as he drags the moisture to my clitoris and rolls it gently, only quickening his pace when I shudder.

I reach out and grab his bare arm as my aching, clenching, and burning body writhes from his touch alone.

"Please," I beg on a whisper, aching to be filled, touched more, something. *Anything.*

When his mouth closes around my pierced nipple and his tongue rolls around it I grip the fur rug and come undone.

My orgasm gently rolls through me in a way I can't control. I've never orgasmed through just clitoral stimulation before and it's insanely amazing. It burns inside in a way that it never has. I feel like I want to fill it but also not because of how crazy it feels.

I hear a click which brings me back to where I am and who I'm with.

I sit up and look at him in the dark, his camera in hand. The sun must have set. I didn't even notice.

His eyes scan my face, my neck, my body. His pupils are dilated in a way I know he's as aroused as I am.

We breathe heavily, staring at each other in a way we haven't before. His surprise mirrors my own. His arousal too.

I watch him start to lean over me, as if readying himself for my kiss.

I'm about to demand he fuck me and forget the foreplay when we both hear a very loud, "Dad? You up there?"

A panicked look comes over his features and I see a realization dawn in his eyes. The same panic and sudden realization comes over me too.

I'm naked in Maddox's dad's room!

I'm not sure he'd approve, in fact, I know he won't. Maddox is the most important person in my life, what am I doing?

"Go," I hiss at him and he stands.

"Coming," he calls to Maddox and finally leaves, giving me one last lingering look from the door.

I scramble to collect my towel and when I'm certain the coast is clear, I slip out of his room and creep all the way downstairs to my own.

Tempest

At breakfast the men are about to leave together, I had thought they'd already gone but it just seems they're both being extra quiet today.

Sargent seems to be even less approachable than usual and I worry that it's because of what happened between us.

I try to sneak past them so I don't have to approach Sargent when last night is still all I can think about. I've never come so hard on somebody before. He manipulated my body with such skill and gentleness that I didn't ever want it to stop.

I'm thinking about it again. I told myself I wouldn't.

"I should be home around three and Dad's giving me an advance so we'll go and get you some new clothes."

I cringe, feeling embarrassed that he had to even say that, especially in front of his dad who already thinks I'm a walking charity case. "Maddox." I stammer to find the right words to follow. "I'm so sorry you feel like you have to provide for me. You should just send me back to England."

"Without me? Not a chance." He grins and I daren't even glance his father's way. "Be ready at three, I'll pick you up."

"You're not taking me shopping, I have clothes enough to last until I earn some more money. Besides, if Devon was being legit, that won't be too much longer."

"You're not working for Devon."

Both Maddox and I look at Sargent who has angrily declared this statement to me. Directly to me.

My eyes catch his which are full of fire and determination.

"Why not?" I ask indignantly. "I need a job and the chance of anybody else hiring me in town when I only have a temporary visa is very minimal."

He looks at his watch and nods at Maddox. "We have to go. We'll discuss this later."

"You can't just tell me what I'm not doing and then walk away. I said yes to the job, it's rude to back out."

He doesn't reply and Maddox only shoots me an apologetic smile before stepping out of the house.

They leave me alone for the day, feeling frustrated.

I do what I can around the house but there's very little to do, so I swim, sunbathe, exercise, ruin exercise by eating crisps, watch a movie, have a shower, and then look around the storage corner in the garage for some paints. I'm itching to get creative. Even if I have to take the paints all the way out to the countryside.

Unfortunately, there are no paints or canvases anywhere.

Maddox returns at three as expected but we don't go into town as he gets a call from an old friend and decides to meet them instead. He does invite me but I don't want to cramp his style, so I assure him it's fine; he can go and when he does I flop down onto the couch face-first and stay there until I fall asleep.

Sargent

Her legs are so long considering how short she seems to me. She's stretched out on her belly on the couch, snoring so gently. Her hair is damp and braided again, it's her signature look. One that suits her.

I remember the days I could sleep like that on a couch and it not bother my body. Even though I'm in great shape, better shape than I was at her age, I couldn't do that now.

I'm about to wake her when she rolls over and tosses her hand over her eyes. Her shirt has risen giving me a glimpse of her stomach. It reminds me of last night and how easily she came undone on my hand. Her stomach tightened and quivered as her orgasm built. That piercing called to me, I needed to feel it, tease it, tease her. God, I'm hard. If Maddox hadn't come home I'd have tossed her onto my bed and ravished her.

I want to right now but she's sleeping.

"Tempest." I whisper the name that suits her so well and crouch beside her in the dark, leaning on one knee on the floor by her shoulder.

My fingers touch her face, tracing the shape of her defined, shapely brows, the smooth curve of her cheekbones, the sharp edge of her jaw, then her lips. My thumb gently pulls on her bottom lip and releases it, making it ping back into place. It trembles with her next breath, making me smile secretly as I trace her chin, the underside, and then place a kiss on the dip in her throat.

I touch another in the space above it, then another, and another until my tongue dares to taste her skin. She's fresh, clean, and smells like soap but she tastes sweet. I suck the lobe of her ear into my mouth when I hear her breath hitch. She's not quite awake but I don't think she's fully sleeping either.

I dare to caress her thigh again, the inside of the leg closest, where her skin is the smoothest.

She starts to whimper in her sleep but it's not the sound of pleasure, it's the sound of pain. There's a distinct change in her body language as she tenses, clamping her thighs down on my hand.

"No, no, please," she begs, and my spine stiffens. I pull my hand from between her thighs as she starts to shake her head, her eyes still closed. "Don't, please. *Please*. Stop."

What the fuck?

"Tempest," I say, louder this time. My hands hover above her as she writhes in her sleep, warding away some unknown monster. "Tempest?"

"No! Let go of me!"

I grab her shoulders and shake until her eyes fly open, tears swimming in them. She blinks rapidly and looks around sleepily but still tearfully. The tears fall as she takes me in, terror slowly melting from her body.

"Are you okay?" I ask softly, unsure on how to approach this.

"Where am I?" she grumbles, pulling herself to sitting so the arm of the couch is at her back. "What time is it?"

"It's a little after nine, I just got home. Are you okay?"

Her lower lip trembles, but not like before. She shakes her head. "No."

I wasn't expecting that answer; most people would lie about their feelings. Not Tempest. "Was it a bad dream?"

"It wasn't a dream," she replies so quietly I hardly hear it. "I'm sorry for worrying you."

"Talk to me," I implore, wanting to take away this pain and turmoil in her eyes. She's normally so happy, if not fiery, but still always happy. "Did somebody hurt you?"

"Yes." Again, I wasn't expecting the honesty.

"Who?"

She wipes her eyes on the back of her hands and replies simply, "It doesn't matter anymore."

I sit on the couch beside her, unsure on whether or not I should reach for her or call Maddox. Instead I think of the only thing I know that could help in this moment. "Tequila?"

Her smile returns but it doesn't meet her eyes. "That will be yet another thing on the list of things I owe you."

That hits me where it hurts because that's not ever how I've felt. "Tempest..."

"No, I mean, I'll pay you back for everything. Honestly. I'm not a freeloader. I've earned every penny I've spent to date. I would never have come if it weren't for having that job and then I got fired. I've never been fired."

She's rambling. How do I make her stop rambling?

More tears fall from her eyes. How do I stop that too?

"And Maddox, he's great, he'll give me as much money as he can but I've never let him. Ask him yourself. I never have and never will take his money, your money... whatever... God... I'm sorry, I don't know what's wrong with me; I'm a mess. I bet this is what you were dreading, seeing me in your hallway I feel so fucking hel—"

God forgive me but she tastes so fucking sweet.

I crush my lips against hers, making her squeak with surprise. Making myself groan as she accepts me so willingly, tangling her tongue with mine perfectly. I grip her around the back of her neck holding her to me as I pull her closer, forcing her to slide her leg over my lap until she's straddling me.

Her fingers push through my hair, it feels incredible and sends tingles down my spine and straight to my dick.

When she releases my mouth for a breath I kiss her throat, her collar, then yank down the front of her shirt, popping out the pierced breast so I can suck it into my mouth.

She gasps, and that goes straight to my cock too.

Her body is so slender in my arms, so light on my lap, so fragile and breakable. I touch her gently, tickling her skin before cupping her rear and lifting her.

We kiss again, our lips connecting clumsily as I carry her to her room, stumbling on my shoes as I kick them off, tripping on my pants as I shove them down when she pushes her bedroom door closed behind us. Reaching over my shoulder with her hand.

I let go of her and she drops to the ground, gasping when I shove her a little harder than intended onto her bed.

She giggles but it stops when I rid her of her shorts, pull her top from over her head and rip her thong from her body with one hand. It snaps. I feel so primal and masculine right now. I've never felt this way before.

"Go easy on the clothing, I literally have none." She smirks at me in the dark and watches me with wild eyes when I stroke myself, standing over her, shirtless, pants off, donning just my CK boxer briefs. The way she takes me in and the way her eyes widen at my size has me chuckling. She's like a little rabbit caught in headlights.

She pulls back as though trying to escape me so I grab her ankle and drag her to the end of the bed. When she laughs again I kneel and kiss her side, tasting each dip of her rib with my tongue and lips. It has her grabbing at my head, jerking and moaning. Jesus, this girl is reacting like a virgin. Has she ever been touched like this?

I push a finger into her to be sure and there's no barrier but fuck she's so tight. Her head falls back as her juices soak my hand and my thumb circles on the hooded little bundle of nerves.

I suck her nipple again and smile when her breathing quickens, her moans get louder and she clenches on my finger. Before she comes I release her, suck my finger into my mouth to taste her. She tastes wild and raw, like pure fucking sweet sin. I dip my finger back inside and kiss her lips. Her legs hang over the edge of the bed as I lay her back onto the mattress.

My free hand, which I'm using to lean on, quickly raises her leg and spreads it as wide as she'll allow.

"What are you doing?" she breathes, panting when I move my hand faster.

Her entire body tenses when I moisten my pinkie finger and slip it down to her puckered exit.

"What are you doing?" Her tone this time is more panicked. "I don't... That's not..."

I claim her mouth again, giving her no time to object as I slip my finger into her tight hole. She tries to bring her legs down but I hook one over my arm and smother her cries with my tongue.

When I allow her to breathe, my pinkie finger buried in her ass up to the knuckle I say, "If I'm only getting you once I want all of you."

"Okay," she replies weakly and covers her eyes with her hand.

I descend on her body, kissing her as I go, keeping a finger in her pulsing, tight, sex and my pinkie in her other as my tongue and lips close over her clit.

"OH! YES! FUCK!" she screams, losing herself.

Oh, she likes it. I love that she likes it. I love that I'm undoubtedly the first man to make her feel this way. I feel smug.

She loses it, climaxing almost instantly. I lap it up as she pulses and shudders. I've never felt a woman get so wet. I want inside of her, right now.

As she's reeling, smiling at the ceiling, I crawl up her body and she cups my face with her hands.

I normally hate that, hate the romantic touches that you only see in movies, hate the kissing of faces, the whispered seductions. But with her it's different, it feels different. It' feels nice, soft, tingly, good.

Her hands are smooth and dainty, and her little moans are incredibly arousing. It all works well together.

We don't speak, both hanging onto the feelings so we don't have to take a moment to think about how this is going to fuck up everything.

I push into her body, watching her take me. There has never been a more erotic moment than the moment the tightest pussy I've ever felt hugs my cock like a vise. Inch by glorious fucking inch she swallows me, enveloping me in moisture and warmth. It burns and tingles. It really fucking burns and tingles.

She grimaces so I stop and kiss her slowly as she adjusts.

"Are you okay?" I whisper, worrying that I might have actually hurt her. Since when did I start to get all sentimental? Normally I'd just give it a moment and then start moving but now the thought of actually hurting her makes me feel things I don't like. "Do you need to stop?"

What am I saying?

"Definitely not," she replies, frowning. "Do you?"

"No."

She looks at me like I'm crazy, "Then what are you waiting for?"

"You're okay?"

"It's been a while, I had to adjust," she replies as I settle my weight on her, my hard dick still buried in her delectable little cunt. This is so fucking taboo and erotic. She's too young for me but in this moment she doesn't feel it. She feels all woman. She is all woman. She has always been all woman.

"How long is a while?"

"A while." She smiles and bites my lower lip. "You can start now, I'm good."

I can't resist, I pull back but her pussy is such a clamp it almost holds me in place. I've never gotten so close to coming so quickly before.

I bury my face in her neck and power through it, gritting my teeth as her fingers dig into my back and her heels dig into the mattress, pushing her hips higher so I can go even deeper.

My body is trembling, almost weak as I fight to hold onto my control. She's so good. She feels so good.

"A little more," I whisper as her mewls get louder and her grip gets tighter. "I really need you to get there." I've never not lasted the length required.

I'm going to blow it and she's going to laugh at the experience with the old man.

Fuck that. I am not old. I have better stamina now than I did in my twenties.

I drive into her faster, my hips hammering at a speed I didn't realize I was capable of.

"God," she whispers, clutching me tighter.

Her pussy starts pulsing around my swollen dick and I know she's there. She shudders with it, crying out so loudly I swallow it with my mouth right before I roar my own release, ramming into her so hard the bed gives an audible creak which it shouldn't do because it's hand fucking carved and built to last!

My orgasm won't end as her walls milk me with her own. It's intense, I lose my vision for a moment and all sense of time.

When I collapse on her as it subsides she squeals so I roll her over, laughing at her glare.

"I forgot how much bigger I am than you," I whisper, brushing her loose hair from her face.

"I don't mind, you're warm. Who needs a blanket?" She curls her body into my chest and I wrap my arms around her.

This isn't something I've done since my ex-wife. Normally I just do the deed and leave but I feel compelled to stay.

No.

I *want* to stay. She smells sweet, my cock is still nestled in her sex, my balls are still tingling and burning, my body is still on fire. I don't want to move an inch.

Her lips touch my chest and she releases a happy little sigh.

"Is sex always like this?"

"No," I reply honestly, wondering if she meant to ask if sex is always like this with me, or just in general. The latter would mean things I don't want to think about or address. "Your pussy is liquid gold." I kiss her temple and roll onto my back, yanking her up to straddle me. Her body flops onto my chest, making me laugh again. "You done?"

"I think I might be." She leans up and winces.

"You're hurt." I frown and immediately remove myself from her body as I roll us back over until she's on her back and I'm hovering above her. "What's wrong? Too rough?"

"No, it's just been a while," she replies gently but her words don't reassure me.

I close my eyes, feeling like shit. "Please tell me I'm not your first."

"No, you're not my first."

Thank fuck.

"You're just my first in a while." Her eyes are happy but sleepy. She yawns, covering her mouth with her arm.

"What does that mean? What's a while?"

She sighs and her body goes limp. Did she just pass out? I give her a little squeeze.

Yep. She is out like a light.

~

Tempest

I wake up in bed, the sun spilling through the windows, my body aching and tense. I look down at my nude body and try to not feel immediate regret but shit... I really messed up.

Oh my God.

I race into the bathroom and turn on the shower. Not because I feel dirty but because I feel dirty.

That makes sense. It does.

I had sex with Sargent. I had sex with Maddox's father.

And he was so good. So so so so so good. Mind-blowing. Amazing. Incredible. PICK AN ADJECTIVE.

OH MY GOD.

I stand under the spray and wait for it to get warm.

I'm going to be limping for days, everything hurts. Especially my insides. His cock is lethal. His strength is lethal.

I want to do it again.

He's twenty years older than me for crying out loud. I wish I'd had sex with an older man sooner.

I smile to myself and practice my reaction when I see him. Perhaps I'll hide in my room for the rest of the day.

My stomach growls. That's not happening.

After my shower I pad to Maddox's room wrapped in a towel and help myself to a top and a pair of boxers. He either stayed out all night or is already up. I hope it's the former. I'm not sure I can look him in the eye right now.

Unfortunately, as I discover as I get close to the kitchen, he's here, chatting with his dad.

Shit.

"Morning," he calls, smiling brightly at me. His hair is a disheveled mess but it suits him. On the beach with a surfboard he'd be every woman's fantasy. All he'd need is a Pepsi, a close-up, and water running down his chest. "Nice top, looks familiar."

"Sorry, I forgot to get my clothes out of the dryer," I reply, keeping my eyes on the refrigerator.

"Morning, Tempest," Sargent says, his voice deep and his tone hiding so many secrets. Or perhaps it's normal and I'm just paranoid?

"Morning," I say but it comes out high-pitched and strange to even my ears.

That was not how I rehearsed it!

I clear my throat and pull open the fridge. "Have you both eaten?"

"Not yet," Maddox replies and at the same time, Sargent says, "Last night."

I blush, I can't help it, my cheeks heat and I want to crawl into a hole.

No. I am not this shy, inconsequential woman. I'm bold and brave, I've traveled the fucking world, to an extent.

I straighten my back and take a deep breath.

"What does everyone want?"

"Let's go out for breakfast. I need to get groceries anyway," Sargent suggests and I notice Maddox shoot him a surprised look in my peripheral vision.

I finally turn, close the refrigerator and look at the man who literally had something in every hole in my body last night.

He winks at me secretly and that blush returns.

"I'll just go and get my clothes." I point to the utility room which is a door on the same wall as the kitchen.

"I need a shower," Maddox says around a mighty yawn.

Sargent, however, is already dressed and ready for the day. That doesn't surprise me. Does the man ever sleep? How does one still look so handsome and put together after last night?

I head into the utility room as planned and start removing the pile of clothing from the dryer straight into a tub. Some are mine, some are theirs. I fold them neatly as I go, placing them in piles on the ground.

As I'm kneeling on the floor, sorting through the tub full of mixed clothing, I feel hands on my hips and hear a belt rattle.

"What are you doing?" I hiss, grabbing at his wrists but his hand pushes mine away and then wraps around my braid. He pushes my face into the clean clothes and parts my thighs.

He presses his bulge into my aching sex.

Hmmm, that feels nice. Even if I am still really achy and sore.

"I want to fuck you again like you wouldn't believe," he

murmurs, stroking my back and yanking me back up to his chest so his large hand can caress and squeeze my breast. "Your body is incredible. Perfection." He bites my neck gently while rubbing my shoulders after releasing my hair and breast. "I said one night, but I need another. Just one more."

His lips move across my hair and neck in a way that has me panting and needy. Who'd have thought having your head and neck kissed and touched in such a way could make you a ball of jelly.

He pulls my hair back with both hands, massaging my head roughly as he grinds his bulge into the curves of my rear.

What is he doing to me?

"I guess we never really said a specific number," I breathe, unable to find my actual voice as I'm too relaxed by his touch.

Twisting my head, he crushes his lips to mine and pushes away from me just as suddenly.

I sag onto the tub like what... the... fuck... just... happened to me?

I want to nap now.

8

Sargent

We drive for an hour before stopping at a favorite restaurant of mine. It doesn't hurt that it's owned by a close acquaintance so we have no trouble getting a table.

I had to sit next to her the entire way here because Maddox decided to be a gentleman and let her ride shotgun. Now I have to sit next to her at the table because there's only three of us and it's unavoidable.

I keep going back to last night in my head, or more aptly this morning, how I need to do it again. I need to fuck her again and again but what Maddox said before has me worrying. She puts her heart into everything.

I need to level it out with her, make sure she understands that this is just sex. This is about two consenting adults finding release with each other. This can't be anything more.

I make a pros and cons list too, just in case she tries to argue with me.

Not that she will. I'm not so big-headed that I think she's

been pining after me. The girl isn't fond of me, I see it in her eyes.

Maddox orders for her when she tries to order the least expensive thing on the menu. Typical. Such a little cliché. Does she not understand that money has never been the issue? I should speak to Maddox about making that clearer.

I insist on not being a part of the conversation for most of it. I let them have their easy friendship without butting in. It's bad enough I've fucked the first girl he's ever brought home regardless of their relationship. Especially when just the day before he decided Devon is too old for her and too much of a dog. I can hardly consider myself any better than Dev. I sleep with different women. There are very few women who I've slept with more than once though I do have a few favorites who I return to.

She's my new one. My new favorite. There are so many more things I want to do to her body.

I remember climbing out of her bed, leaving her tangled in the sheets, the scent of our deed still lingering in the air and on her skin. For a moment I hadn't wanted to leave her but then I brushed that shit right off.

My phone rings and Devon's name blinks in the middle of the screen.

"Excuse me," I say to Maddox and Tempest.

They both continue with their quiet conversation, laughing under their breath like school children not adults.

"Yes?"

"You sound cheery this morning," Devon replies sarcastically and I know he's grinning. He's always been a fan of my moods. Lord knows why.

"I've just finished breakfast with my son and his guest."

Her eyes cut to me but I ignore her look of what could be shame mixed with pain. It was so fleeting it was hard to tell.

I don't owe her anything anymore than she owes me something. She's lived with us for long enough to know I'm a bastard in all sense of the word.

"Ah, she still teasing you with those perky breasts?"

I sigh heavily and warn, "Devon. Your point?"

He laughs hard. "Relax, brother from another mother. I'm just calling to see if little Miss Perky is still interested in that job."

"No, she is not," I grit, the thought of her working in close proximity to him is making me feel like I want to clock him in his face with a powerful right hook.

"Funny, that's not what Maddox said."

I turn away to give myself some semblance of privacy as their eyes come to me again and their conversation slows to a stop. "If you already asked, then why ask again?"

"Just working on a theory," he replies cheerfully. "If you like her, you should just say. I'll back off."

"Have at it," I reply and hang up my phone. I look at them both and they both look away. "Maddox, when are you getting your hair cut?"

He rolls his palm over the thick, long tresses and grins. "When I feel like it."

"You look like a stoner."

"He is a stoner," Tempest mutters and Maddox shoves her

so hard she falls off her chair with a squeal and nearly brings the table down with her.

He laughs so hard he can't breathe, Tempest however, climbs back into her seat with bright red cheeks. I'm torn between being mortified by their childish behavior and laughing because she really did go down quite easily.

When she catches me smiling her eyes narrow which only makes me smile more.

"Behave," I tell my son when the eyes of others come to us. When he stops laughing and she perks up again, I ask, "What do you both have planned for today?"

"We are dropping Pest off at Dev's, then I'm going to finish inventory."

I ignore the first part. "You're working very hard, I'm pleasantly surprised."

"Maddox never does a job half-arsed." Tempest smiles warmly at my son and I wonder how I could ever have mistaken their affections for anything other than familial. There's no chemistry between them on the romantic scale.

There's definitely chemistry between the two of us.

I still need to have a talk with Maddox about his intentions though. His feelings could change and I don't want to come between them if they do.

Although I wonder if he'll want anything to do with her should he find out I've been inside of her body. It does make for an odd predicament.

Which brings me to my next thought. Birth control. We didn't use preventative measures at all. I don't think she's on anything either.

I feel sick. Why is this only now crossing my mind? I don't want to be a father again at forty. Jesus fucking Christ... I'm too old to be making these kinds of mistakes. That must also be why it felt so intense with her. I always use protection, always. It's not because she has an incredible pussy, it's because it has been years since I rode a girl bareback.

I am such a fool.

If my mood wasn't bad before it is now.

Tempest

I start my new job this morning. To say I'm excited would be an understatement.

"I'll drop Tempest at Devon's Shack," Sargent insists. "I need to have a word with Devon anyway."

A look of understanding passes between the men. They seem to be silently speaking with their eyes.

Whatever. I just hope Sargent's mood elevates during the journey there. Throughout breakfast he just seemed to spiral deeper and deeper into this pit of anger. Maddox noticed it too but neither of us said anything.

Maddox gets an Uber to work or home to pick up a car. I'm not sure, I didn't ask, I just let Sargent hold open the door of the SUV for me, close it after me and then make his way to his side.

As soon as he drives us out of the carpark and onto the busy street he says two words that have me panicking like a teenager. "Birth control."

"What... what about it?" I stammer, ignoring the heavy beating of my heart.

"Are you on birth control?"

Fuck. Shit. Bollocks. Wank.

I close my eyes and calm my breathing, trying not to mentally chastise myself too badly. "No. I'm not."

He slams his hand against the steering wheel, making me jump. "Shit."

"I'm not pregnant, I'm not ovulating," I assure him. "But we should really use condoms in future."

"No future," he declares quickly. "No more. Whatever happened, it can't happen again."

I try not to feel too hurt by that but it doesn't seem fair. "Why?"

"Because I don't make mistakes like that."

Okay, this time I cannot hide my hurt because, ouch. "Well, at least I know where I stand."

"That's not—"

I cut him off, "Perhaps you could refrain from accosting me in the utility room should you not wish to pursue this further."

I see a muscle tick in his jaw as his handsome profile and blue eyes pierce the road ahead.

He doesn't reply and I don't push him for a response. What's the point?

"Thank you for giving me a ride to work," I say softly, trying to portray that whatever happened between us there are no hard feelings. He doesn't reply and that pisses me off. We tangoed together. I didn't tell him to ditch the condoms. "If you want me to get the morning-after pill, or something, I will. I'm not trying to trap you with some pregnancy I don't want. Okay? I want to go back to traveling. I can't do that with a kid." He still doesn't reply. "But you'll have to book it and pay for it because I don't have the money and I don't know any local doctors that will supply the pill."

"How is your sexual health?" He keeps his tone casual, it doesn't stop me from bristling at his words though.

"How's yours?"

"I was tested two months ago. I'm vigilant," he replies, looking at me briefly. "I have to be because I fuck a different woman every week, but I always use protection."

He fucks a different woman every week. Jesus. I'm just a number to him, aren't I?

"You?" he asks cautiously.

"I'm clean."

"That's not what I was asking."

"You want to know the last time I had sex? That's really none of your business."

"It is if it puts my health at risk."

"I have sex with a different guy every week too," I lie, not wanting to seem virginal, prudish, and pathetic. "But I use protection."

His lips twitch as though my words amuse him. "So why did you tell me it had been a while?"

"It's been a couple of months." Die with the lie, I chant, having learned it from a movie. "That's a while for me. I normally don't go more than three days."

I am so full of shit.

His eyes which held amusement are now blank and devoid of emotion. Or perhaps I'm not reading him well enough.

"My son seems to think otherwise, he warned me to keep Devon away from you. Said you're not like other women and you put your heart into things."

"Maddox doesn't like it when I sleep around. He's too much of a gentleman," I respond, mumbling now. "I don't want to talk anymore."

"Devon is your type?" I see his hands clench the steering wheel.

"I don't have a type. If I want it, I take it."

"It's that simple?"

"It really is."

He rolls his eyes. "Your parents must be so proud."

What a condescending shit! "So must yours be!"

"Mine are in another state stewing over past arguments, they're not anything."

"Mine are dead, isn't life a bitch?" I reply bitterly and cross my arms over my chest.

His lips pinch together and I see his regret immediately as he replies, "I'm sorry, Tempest. I didn't mean..."

"It's fine, I got over them a long time ago." I look out of the window. "Can you stop talking to me now? I prefer your silence."

Sargent

I've never been a particularly sensitive guy. I often miss compassionate social cues so it's not surprising I'm sitting here beside her, silent as she asked. I don't know what to say or do to rectify my mistake.

I didn't know her parents were dead. I never asked about her family.

Maybe I should?

No. It's none of my business. Just like her sex life isn't any of my business.

I pull into the parking lot outside of Devon's Shack which is a place where people can buy or rent all kinds of equipment for the beach. They also teach surfing, jet skiing, skating, etc.

I hate bringing her here. I should have offered her a job myself but she'd never take it and to be honest I don't need her around me anymore than she already is. We would not work well together.

"You came!" Devon calls when we step into the shack, and she finally starts smiling. She's never smiled at me like that, so happy and easy. I get a nagging hum in my chest but mentally lock it away. I don't know what it was and I don't care to know.

"You look beautiful, but if it's okay, we have a uniform that all employees must wear." Devon, without touching her, guides her to the staff rooms, passing other members who wave and smile curiously as we go.

He leads her to a rail of uniforms on the back wall which comprise of black T-shirts with the store logo and tight, Lycra cut-offs that stop below the knee. "At the end of each day you chuck them into the bin in the corner and we have them washed and ready for the next day. Write your name in the label and you won't get mixed up."

I watch her take her clothes into one of the few changing rooms and Dev claps me on the back.

"Don't worry, I'll take good care of her."

"Keep that in your pants or Maddox will make my life hell," I hiss, pointing at his dick which is visible through his own Lycra cut-offs.

He chuckles and rolls his eyes. "You sure Maddox is the only reason I should keep it to myself?"

My eyes narrow but he only laughs harder.

"I promise, unless she makes a move, I won't touch her."

"Even *if* she does, you won't touch her," I correct and his smile fades.

"Bit possessive there, Wolf. Want to talk about it?"

"Nothing to talk about, so long as we're clear."

His smile returns but it's menacing. "Like I said, you lay claim, I'm off that. You don't, I'm on that should she wish it. I'm not pushing anything on her but I won't say no if she offers. You've seen her, she's sweet. I'd be a fool to say no."

My jaw aches with how tightly it's clenched. "If you make her uncomfortable..."

"Not my style, you know that. Don't need to harass a woman to get in her pants. I can dot my I's and cross my t's. Not hard to know when a woman isn't interested."

She exits the changing room and I have to bite back a groan at those pants. They cover everything but also show everything.

"You sure don't look like you're not interested," Devon mutters so only I hear. Then he twirls her under his arm. "Beautiful. Now, why don't I show you the ropes and get you started?"

"Thanks for the ride," she says to me, her tone quiet and sweet.

I hand her my business card because she doesn't have my number. "Call me when you're finished and I'll pick you up or send somebody."

That's my guilt for bringing her dead parents into it shining through.

"It's fine, I can handle it. I need to pick up those photos from you later anyway."

"What photos?" she blurts and I see her panic and mistrust aimed directly at me.

I also see Devon's brow rise. This asshole does not miss a beat. "Just some old photographs he's edited and printed for me from back in the day."

Did she really think I'd betray her trust like that?

I haven't even looked at the images yet myself, let alone showed them to anybody.

We hear a bang and Dev sighs, "Duty calls. Come on, Pest, let's show you the ropes."

Tempest

Everybody is so lovely. They have a strict sexual harassment policy too which means if some jerk grabs me like that Cap guy in the diner then I get to fuck him up and it's all good.

I make fast friends with a girl who is just a year older than me. Her name is Sadie and she's lovely but definitely on the geek side. I learn that she loves to watch Anime as much as she loves to surf and she adores science and diving.

Her enthusiasm for everything makes me feel as though I am constantly miserable.

Devon realizes we get along and leaves her to show me the ropes.

I had assumed this would be an admin role but Devon tells me he thinks I'll do better on the shop floor. Apparently, I'm charming.

I wax boards, help people carry them to their cars, make sure the shelves are stocked and keep an eye on potential shoplifters.

Everybody is so pleasant, the beach dwellers are friendly and calm, there are so many dogs too I lose count during my break where Devon takes me next door to the café and treats me to an iced tea and an egg salad sandwich.

He's a really nice guy and not nearly as perverted as I initially thought. If anything, he's extremely respectful of my boundaries and very supportive of me as a woman. He declares he's for equality and feminism though he could just be saying that because he wants to get me into bed.

At sunset, he nods for me to follow, waits for me to change and then leads me to his white Bentley which is parked in a private garage just around the corner.

"You did really well today, I'm impressed with your work ethic." He smiles ahead, showing white, straight teeth that stand out amongst his dark lips and skin. "I'm going to work you in on the schedule for the next couple of weeks. Are there any days you can't do?"

I shake my head. "I'm free, thank you for the opportunity. I've been going out of my mind with boredom."

"You don't strike me as the kind of woman who likes to sit still, that's why I put you on the shop floor instead. You'll rotate with the crew. I like to give them all time in different areas so they don't get bored. We need to sort out your health insurance too but I'm not sure how that will work with your temp visa."

I wince. "It's complicated, I know, I'm sorry."

"Don't apologize, it's nothing we can't handle." He smiles so kindly I feel at ease in a way I haven't all day. "So, did you end up drawing the stiff?"

"The stiff?"

"Sargent."

My lips form an O. "Oh.... No, not yet."

"Well if you need another model I'd be happy to oblige." He grins playfully.

My inner artist overrides my need to keep a distance from my boss. "You would?"

His grin becomes a smile as he replies, "Of course. So long as I get a copy of the end results. I'm a big fan of art and I think your idea; The Divine Skin was it?" I nod and he continues, "Is superb. I know Sargent thinks so too."

"Will you really pose? You won't be all weird around me afterwards?"

"If I started acting weird around every woman who has seen me naked, I'd never be normal." He clears his throat as I stifle my laugh. "That sounded better in my head."

I throw my head back and laugh as he pulls to a stop outside my temporary home. "Let me get some new pencils and some more paper for my sketchbook and we'll set a date."

"Sounds perfect," he replies, winking at me as I climb out of the car.

"Thank you for bringing me," I say before closing the door behind me and all but skipping to the house.

I immediately race to my journal and jot this amazing day down, then I pull out my sketchbook and my last pencil. It's dark and smudges well but it's not the best pencil I've used.

Maybe soon I'll be able to start sketching and painting again. Not long now until I get paid. He said the end of the month and it's the middle so I shall be counting down the days. This is going to be epic.

9

Sargent

I find Maddox in the break room, speaking to some of the people we work with. He gets along with them so well, his moods nothing like my own and I wonder if I've allowed myself to be consumed by bitterness. Or perhaps I'm just a bastard.

"Boss is here," a woman mutters and they scarper, all but Maddox who greets me with a smile.

"I was wondering when you'd get here," he pours himself a coffee at the machine and offers me one but I decline. "How'd she get on? Did you have a word with Devon?"

"She was fine and yes, I did."

"What did he say?"

I lick my lip, wondering how to approach the subject without implicating myself. I'm simply testing the waters.

"He seemed to think I was saying it because I want the girl." I say this as flippantly as possible.

His eyes darken with a scowl. "So he saw her as a challenge?"

He clearly trusts me to not do anything with her or he'd have asked me if it were true. Christ, I'm a fucking cunt.

"Possibly, but he said he'll leave her be," I reply. "Unless she makes the first move."

"She won't," he murmurs, more to himself than to me.

I blow out a breath. "Why are you concerning yourself with her sex life?"

"She's my best friend, am I not supposed to?"

"Feels like a more than friendly gesture to me." Why am I pushing this?

"Dad..."

"I'm just suggesting that maybe you think and feel more for her than you'd care to admit?"

He places his cup angrily on the side. "Don't go putting shit in my head. She's family to me. I don't want to lose her."

"I just don't get it, she's young, adventurous, artistic, calm," I list off her qualities and wonder when I noticed these things about her. "She's sexy..."

"She's my friend, don't call her sexy, Dad, that's weird. She's young enough to be your daughter."

The look he gives me is a clear warning. Too late for that.

"You're honestly telling me you don't feel anything? Women like her don't just appear around every corner. If I were your age..."

What am I saying?

"Dad," he groans, rolling his eyes. "We're friends."

"I'm just saying," I reply, holding up my hands defensively. "She'll move on eventually."

"Dad, she doesn't like me like that either. She can move on all she likes."

I shrug like I don't care, which I shouldn't care, but I also do. His feelings are the only feelings I care about.

"So, really, you don't care if she and Devon..."

He shoots me a look and interrupts, "Are you trying to campaign for your friend? She's my age, Dad. She's not like other women. She doesn't just fuck anybody. I know that because I traveled with her for a year and she never once looked at another guy. She never once looked at me."

So she *was* lying when she said that shit to me this morning. I had a feeling she was.

"Leave her alone, both of you. If I find out either of you have done something to make her uncomfortable I will never speak to you again."

Shit. I let that escalate but at least now I know where I stand with him were he to find out about what happened.

Tempest

The next morning, I creep into Maddox's room and find him sitting on the rug, cross-legged, looking at an image of a ship and a bunch of papers with numbers and lists on them.

He looks stressed and thoroughly confused.

"Made a mistake?" I ask, sitting on his bed and picking up his phone to play a game.

He shrugs and then stretches his neck. I wonder how long he has been sitting here.

I put his phone down, shift to sitting behind him and start rubbing his neck.

He groans and lets his head fall forwards.

"What's wrong?"

"I counted an extra crate on the last two freights I released."

I keep rubbing, digging my fingers into the tight spots on his neck. "That's not your job is it?"

"No, but you know I like to be thorough."

"But if it's not your job, there's a chance you're missing something. Have you spoken to the person who runs that department?"

"No," he grumbles and then sighs heavily, resting back against my knees and dropping his head in my lap so I can massage his forehead and scalp. "That would probably be a good idea wouldn't it?"

"Yes," I reply, leaning down to kiss his jaw.

He smiles and rolls away. "It doesn't feel right."

"Then tell your dad."

"No," he blurts, gathering the paper. "I want to handle this myself."

"Show him what you're made of?"

"Exactly." He grins, scratching the stubble on his chin. "I've got this."

"I have no doubt you do."

I watch as he yanks his shirt off over his head and for the first time since we became friends, I start to feel awkward. This is all Sargent's fault.

"How was your first day?"

"It was incredible. Devon has offered to let me draw him!"

He gives me a scowl when he pulls a clean shirt on, hiding his muscles from my view. Not that I was looking. "I bet he has."

"What's that tone for?" I giggle nervously and flop back onto his bed. "It's all for art."

"Does he know that?"

"Would it matter if he didn't?" I remark playfully and his scowl deepens. "Don't be like that."

"I don't want him taking advantage. He's a shit when it comes to women."

I close my eyes but my smile doesn't vanish. "You sound jealous. Do you want a piece of him instead?"

When his dirty sleep shirt hits me in the face I squeal and throw it back.

"I'll keep away if you like him," I jest. "Just say the word... ACK!"

He dives on me and I know what's coming before he starts. He licks his hands and as I battle to keep him away, he rubs one on my face and then the other.

"You arse!" I yell, twisting under him as he straddles me and laughs at my disgust. "Let go."

I buck him off but we both tumble from the bed and onto the floor with a thud. I land on him so I'm fine but he looks a bit dazed.

I use this moment to my advantage and straddle him like he just did to me.

He laughs uncontrollable, his chest heaving and his eyes squeezing shut as I dig my fingertips into his sides.

"Stop," he begs but that's not our magic word. He tries to grab my wrists but I twist them this way and that, keeping them out of his hold.

Suddenly his demeanor changes, he stops laughing and his body goes still.

"Stop," he says firmly this time.

"Nope," I laugh, still tickling him.

"I said stop!" he yells and with a strength he's never used on me before he rolls me over and pins me down, my hands above my head.

"What's wrong?" I ask, noticing the look in his eyes as one I've not seen before.

His chest heaves aggressively as he tries to catch his breath.

"Nothing," he murmurs and smiles sweetly at me. "I thought I was going to pee myself."

"Urrrp," I laugh dramatically while pretending to vomit. Then I feel something else. Something I didn't notice until I shifted in a way that has it pressing directly between my parted thighs. "You have a boner."

"Yeah," he murmurs, scrunching his face up in disgust. "It's been a while since I got laid and you were wriggling on top of it... there's only so much stimulation it can take before it starts to say hello."

I have no words. This has never happened before. I've seen him get morning wood but never has he reacted this way to me. Or if he has, he's hidden it well.

We just stay on the floor, him still between my thighs, my arms still pinned above my head.

"You need to move," I whisper.

He grinds against me and groans, a tingle shoots up my spine. Of course it feels good. He's stimulating an area that is supposed to feel good.

"Not like that!" I screech, staring into his dilated pupils.

He starts laughing and collapses on top of me, crushing me into the ground.

"Dude, you are crossing so many boundaries right now."

"I'm sorry," he says genuinely and with a smile on his face he climbs off my body and covers himself with his hands. "Are you okay?" I nod. "Are we okay?"

"Of course," I reply, standing and looking at him as he grabs the pillow from his bed and places it over his thing when he sits down. "Is this suddenly weird between us?"

He shakes his head. "Definitely not. I'll jerk off to some porn and go get laid this weekend. My body doesn't know we're friends and my dad was saying all this shit to me yesterday that has only succeeded in confusing me."

I try not to panic at that and ask, "What shit?"

"He just pointed out all the reasons you're basically marriage material." He looks as though he's gauging my reaction so I make a point to not react. "But we're us. Marriage, sex, kids, that'll all ruin everything."

I hum my agreement and move toward the door. "Tell your dad to stay out of our business."

"I will."

"We're best friends, Mad," I call over my shoulder. "I can't lose you."

"You won't."

What the fuck is his dad doing? Is he not content with

playing with me that now he has to bring his son into the equation too?

Sargent

I woke up when I heard Maddox leave. That boy does work hard. I don't have to work as much because of the slack he's picking up, that and I'm boss. Most of that shit is done for me.

I brush my teeth, shower, and when I re-enter my room, there's a very perturbed-looking Tempest waiting for me.

She's truly beautiful today. Her hair is damp and hanging over her shoulders, her nipples are visible through the fabric of her white shirt. I should give her my card to buy new clothing but then I wouldn't get to see her perky round tits nearly every day.

Her greenish-hazel eyes are alight with her anger but that doesn't stop her from getting a good look at my bare chest.

I hold onto the towel around my waist with one hand as I use my other hand to push my hair back.

"What can I do for you, Temptress?" I ask and her eyes flicker to mine and narrow.

"Maddox got a boner this morning."

Ew. "Okay, didn't need to know that."

"Well, it's all your fucking fault." Her glare is a powerful one but I can't stop thinking about my son and his... NOPE. "Why did you have to go and open your big mouth?"

"What are you talking about?"

"He told me what you said, he said it's confusing him. We were play fighting like we *always* do and he got a fucking boner." She's really mad about this. "He's my friend. I can't lose him. Why did you have to say anything?"

I take a step toward her. "I just wanted to see how he felt about you." That's the truth too, sort of. It's a half-truth.

"Why?"

"So when we fuck, he's not getting hurt," I reply. "Unfortunately, he told me to stay away from you."

"Good," she replies, folding her arms across her chest which only makes her nipples stick out more.

Groan.

"Because we're never having sex again."

"Yesterday I was inclined to believe that too but today is a new day."

Her mouth drops open. "I'm not having sex with you. I don't even know what I was thinki— Pick your towel back up."

I look down at the towel around my ankles and grin. "Oops."

"No, we aren't doing this," she snarls and sounds serious so I sigh and pick up my towel like she said. "I have plans soon."

"Oh?"

"Devon just called." She raises a brow, she's goading me. It's not working. Just because I want to jab him in his dick doesn't mean it's working. "I'm going to draw him today."

My hand that isn't holding my towel clenches into a fist but my face remains stoic. "Sorry, what?"

"He's taking me to buy some new pencils and then I'm going to draw him."

I stare at her, waiting for her to laugh and declare that she's kidding. She doesn't.

"Naked? You're going to draw him naked?" I ask because I just need her to clarify.

"Yes."

"Absolutely not."

She laughs humorlessly. The sound grates on my nerves. "I don't think you have a say in the matter."

"Are you sure?"

"I'm sure." Her eyes widen when I drop my towel again, revealing my rather solid cock.

"Don't," she whines, backing up as I prowl toward her. "Sarge..."

At the last second, I turn away and reach for my closet door.

She lets out a breath and watches me dress. She wants me.

"I'm not one to stand in the way of art, when I can spectate," I say, turning to her in just my boxers. "What say you?"

"You're coming with us?"

I nod once. "Yep."

"I... he..." She looks around, trying to find some excuse. "I was lying."

I raise a brow as I assess the truth in this admittance. "You're not going to draw him?"

"Not today, I mean... he offered and I said I would but we didn't make any plans. I just wanted to..."

"See how I'd react?" Is she testing theories or being childish? I don't care for it.

She nods once much like I did and turns to the door.

"Don't play games with me, Pest, I'm too old for that shit."

"Stop saying shit to Maddox then, okay?"

"He's my son, I'll say whatever I choose."

"You're going to ruin everything!"

I shake my head as disbelief courses through me. "You're as foolish as he is. He's likely the best man you will ever meet and you're fooling yourself if you think you'll stay friends forever."

"Why do you want me with him so badly when I know you don't even like me? You're so confusing. How can you admit you want to fuck me in the same chapter that you say you want me with your son?"

She has me there. "I didn't say I wanted you with my son."

"Then what are you saying?"

"I'm saying I need to know where I stand in this cute little threesome so I can fuck you without worrying about ruining my son's life!" I'm yelling. Shit. She just brings out the worst in me.

"I don't want to fuck you so your problem is solved *and* you can stay the fuck out of my—"

That sounded more like a challenge to me so I clamp my lips down on hers before she reaches the end of her sentence.

"Sargent!" she yells, shoving me away but I see the arousal in her eyes and raise a challenging brow. "You're worried where you stand yet you're still trying to do this?"

"What's one more time?" I reply, grabbing her and forcing her over my bed. "Tell me to stop right now and I'll stop."

When she doesn't a surge of masculine pride moves through my body and straight to my cock and my hands yank down her bottoms. I massage her rear, smoothing my palms over her smooth skin before cupping her around the front and finding her clit as my angry cock sinks into her wanting pussy.

A groan leaves me, one that translates just how amazing she fucking feels.

"Why, don't, we..." I pant between thrusts and then stop because she arches back and it moves me in a way that has me teetering on the edge already. "Just take this one day at a time? And fuck until we tire of each other?"

"So... friends with benefits?"

"Minus the friends part."

She glares at me over her shoulder. "You're such an arse. Why don't you like me? What have I ever done to you?"

"I don't like anybody, angel," I reply. "But we don't have to like each other to enjoy this." I start to thrust slowly again and her eyes gently close. "Let's take advantage of it while we can."

"Birth control," she murmurs and I'm elated that she didn't say no.

"Birth control," I repeat in agreement and wind her braid around my hand, figuring one more time bareback won't hurt if she's getting the morning-after pill anyway. "Hold tight, angel."

"To what?"

She gasps when I slam into her so hard she shoots forward, face-planting the mattress. I laugh, but only for a second as she starts to quiver around my hard dick that's still firmly inside of her tight little cunt. She's so wet, making it hard to manipulate her clit in the right way. Though I know I must be doing it right because she's mewling like a fucking porn star and her entire body is shaking.

I pump slowly, circling my hips and then jackhammering into her quickly until I feel her nearing the edge. I'm teasing her but I love it. Her little curses and whimpers and moans are fuel to my already heated fire.

When I lose it, it's seconds after her and it's maybe even more intense than the other night. She feels so good I can't stop, not until we're both so sore and tired it's all we can do not to pass out.

The next day, as promised, we go to my doctor and get her the morning-after pill which she takes with ease, he tests us both for diseases and books her in to get the IUD as was her request. We also get more condoms than I can count of all varieties to last us until that appointment. I'm not sure it'll be enough.

10

Tempest

"What's that?" Maddox asks.

It's the weekend and it has been a seriously long week at work. I have to leave in less than five minutes and Maddox is taking me.

When I've been home from work and Maddox has been occupied or working himself, I've been in the arms of his father. Who, during the times we aren't fucking, acts like I don't exist. But during the times we are, fucks me like it's his last time.

"It's nothing," Sargent replies, unable to look me in the eyes as he passes.

Maddox has just opened the door and there's a man there with a clipboard in his hands and a van parked behind him. "New furniture?" he asks, trailing after his dad.

"No."

"Sex toys?"

"Son," Sargent snaps when the man with the clipboard starts laughing. "Take her to work before she's late."

"I'm on it." Maddox winds an arm around my shoulders as

my eyes finally meets Sargent's. He's not happy that Maddox has me so close but what can he do? He's my best friend and thankfully, since the incident with the boner last week, things have returned to normal. "Need me to pick you up?"

"I'll let you know," I reply softly, smiling up at him. "How is work? You look less stressed."

"You were right about the crate issue. It's resolved. It was just for emergency deliveries. Every cargo ship has one."

I wind my arm around his back and grin. "Told you not to worry." I look back again at Sargent as I climb into the waiting SUV. He gives me a small smile and nods for me to go. What's in the van, I wonder?

"I think my dad is taking pictures again. He was in the dark room this morning at like six."

I tense and look at my friend. "He was?"

"Yep. And his cameras aren't where they usually are."

"Huh," I reply. "Did you ask him about it?"

"Nah, I don't want to scare him off. It might be a private project."

"What makes you think that?"

"I tried to get in there when you got up and he was in the bathroom but the door was locked. It's never locked."

Thank heavens. "He'll show you when he's ready."

"And now this delivery... it has one wondering..."

"Stop being nosy." I giggle and slap his arm.

He feigns injury and pretends to swerve the car to the side. "I'm driving, you ass."

"You're driving my arse?" I retort. "That's just dirty."

He slaps me back, hard, it misses my arm and gets me in

the diaphragm. So naturally, like any other good friend; I pretend that I can't breathe, as though he's knocked the wind out of me.

"Shit," he curses, pulling to the side of the road and turning to face me. "Are you okay?"

"I... need..." I grab the back of his head, pull him closer and as he nears with worried eyes, I lick the side of his face with a very wet tongue.

"You nasty little bitch," he laughs, sitting back and wiping my spit off his face.

I grin and look at the cars passing us on the road. "Get driving or I'm going to be late."

"SHIT!" we both scream when a man suddenly slams his hands against his side of the car.

His black eyes glare right at me and he taps a finger pad against the glass so hard his finger bends backwards. "You! I know you!"

"Oh my God," I breathe. Laughing at the state of the asshole whose nose I broke. "It's Cap guy."

"I should get out and kick your ass," Maddox snarls at him as I lean around him and give the prick my middle finger.

"Have a bath, you dirty fuck, you stink!" I shout at him, keeping my middle finger in his sight as Maddox pulls away.

I laugh with my friend as we put the carpark and the greasy guy behind us.

"What a loser." Maddox sighs, shaking his head. Then he starts laughing again. "You dirty fuck...? That's a new insult for you."

"It was the first thing that came to my head."

He squeezes my thigh. "I'd have kicked his ass, but you're going to be late for work."

"It's fine." I grin as I awkwardly take his hand off my thigh and place it back on the console. He's never touched me like that before. It felt different. Or perhaps I'm reading into it. "I think breaking his nose was enough of a punishment."

"That was badass."

"I'm glad you think so."

When his hand goes back to my thigh, I bite my lip but leave it be. It's an intimate touch that I'm not sure how to deal with because it's Maddox and Maddox doesn't touch me intimately. We're friends and that's it.

I mean... I'm fucking his dad.

This is getting complicated. I need to tell him. I need to speak to Sargent about telling him.

Sargent

It's done. I admire my handiwork. Clear plastic sheeting is carefully tacked to the wall and ground. An easel stands in the center of it, big enough to hold a rather large canvas. There's a chest full of shelves that pull up, housing many different kinds of paints. I'm not sure what she favors so I bought them all.

There are also sketch pads of all sizes and pencils of all types and qualities.

It's past the firepit, far enough away from the pool but not so far that she can't see it.

I hope she likes it. Though I think I've done too much. There's even an optional gazebo hood that will protect her from the sun if necessary.

It is too much.

I'm starting to panic.

I don't do this. I don't give gifts and make nice gestures.

Who am I anymore and what is this girl doing to me?

When I'm about to tear it all down, I hear a car pull up in the driveway. It sounds a lot like Devon's but I don't want to make assumptions. My heart is already hammering in my chest.

Why did I think any of this would be a good idea?

I enter the house through the back door and move to the front one. There's a knock so I know it's not Devon and Tempest.

I peek through the blinds and blink at what I'm seeing.

"What the fuck?" I breathe and yank open the door. "Absolutely fucking not. Get back in your shit car and fuck off."

"But I want to see my son!"

Tempest

Devon drops me off, walks me to the door and follows me in without invitation. I suppose if he and Sargent are as close as what he says then it's okay. Also he seemed really disturbed when we passed an old, gray car in the long driveway.

The second we both step inside I hear something smash and

Devon curses and pushes me behind him. I watch as Sargent drags a flailing, screeching woman toward the door.

"MY SON!" she screams, frothing at the mouth as her brown eyes scan the area and her long, pale, chubby limbs flail.

"That's Mad's mum," I whisper and the second her eyes come to me she stops flailing and screaming and drops like a dead weight.

Sargent drops her, nobody can hang onto a dead weight if they aren't expecting it.

"What the fuck are you doing in my house?" she screeches at me, coming straight for me with clawed fingers outstretched. Devon pulls me back out of her grasp, literally lifting me off the ground and turning us both. "WHO IS SHE, SARGENT?"

"She high?" Devon asks Sargent as he wrestles with her again.

I see three angry scratch marks down his neck and rage bubbles in my gut.

"Help me toss her out," Sargent says as the woman hisses, spits, and sobs.

"Who the fuck is she?" she screams, clearly off her head.

"She is none of your business, you psychotic bitch," Devon yells, grabbing her kicking ankles as Sargent grabs her arms.

Unfortunately, in her haste to escape, she brings her booted foot into Devon's groin and he goes down like a sack of potatoes off a shelf.

"Oooh," I hiss, cringing with him as he tries not to vomit from the pain.

I rush to him, ready to help when a stench I can't describe fills my nostrils and a blur of graying, brown hair is in my face.

We tumble to the ground and I push against her, trying to find leverage.

I feel her teeth sink into my shoulder and scream. This bitch really is crazy!

"I will end you! You homewrecking whore!" she screeches at me, her wild eyes enraged.

"Get her off me or I'm going to lose my shit!" I yell, pushing at her face with my hand as my knee goes to her belly.

"ENOUGH!" Sargent bellows, grabbing her and literally throwing her into the door. "Call the cops, she is cracked out of her fucking mind." He slams her onto the ground and pins her with both arms behind her back as I fumble with the phone in the hall. Ignoring the pain in my arm as I dial and speak to the dispatcher.

They can hear her wailing like a banshee.

Everybody this side of the world can likely hear her wailing like a banshee.

"I thought you were clean, Kelly." Sargent sighs, frowning at the woman who was once his wife. It's hard to imagine a man like him ever being with a woman like her. She's a mess. She looks bloated, sickly, her hair is graying and patchy. She has cuts up and down her bare arms from where she's been picking them and scratching.

When I hang up the phone I race to grab Devon a bag of ice from the freezer. He accepts it gratefully, still in agony. I'm wondering if I should have called an ambulance too.

"Are you okay?" I ask Sargent as she finally stills and just sobs beneath him.

He nods and smiles at me gently. "Are you?"

I look at my arm, the skin isn't broken but I go in search of some peroxide anyway. When I find it, I clean the wound and open the door for the cops to come in.

"I'll just..." Devon carries himself to the sofa and collapses onto it. Poor bloke.

"I'll get you some pain killers." I look at Sargent as the local sheriffs handcuff the bitch in question. "You got this?"

He nods and deals with that while I deal with his friend.

There are stools on the ground and a broken glass is scattered around the far wall as though it has been thrown.

An hour passes, the cops take our statements and leave, Devon hobbles to his car, and I finish clearing away any glass. I can't believe that just happened. That was insane.

I'm still in shock I think.

The bitch bit me. She hasn't been with Sargent since Maddox was fourteen. Maddox said so himself.

So why did she feel territorial? Was it the drugs? I knew she was a heavy addict but I didn't know to what extent. Now I'm wondering if Maddox knows to what extent.

"You didn't have to do that," Sarge says softly as he sinks onto the sofa and covers his face with his hands.

"I don't mind," I reply, wiping the mark off the white wall where the liquid from inside the glass splattered. "It's probably going to need repainting."

"If only you could paint over bad memories," he mutters and looks at me through hooded eyes. "Come here."

I drop the rag and move to him, taking his outstretched hand in mine.

He pulls me onto his lap until I'm straddling him and gently touches the bite mark which mars a blank space of my tattoo.

"She's a fucking bitch," he growls, kissing the space beside the mark gently as though his touch will make it all better. I'm surprised when it does.

I thread my fingers together behind his neck and kiss him softly.

We don't ever kiss softly. We fuck each other's mouths. We don't make out like passionate lovers. What we do is brutal and painful in the best way, but right now this is sweet and calm in a new way.

He grips my hips and sits up so our bodies are flush together and my groin is against him. "Are you okay?"

I nod and he lifts me and presses my back to the couch. "I'm just sorry I couldn't do more to help. I didn't have an opening."

"When she's like that she's strong. I'm sorry I let her get close enough to do this to begin with," he whispers, kissing my shoulder again. He rests his body on mine and looks down at me with a gaze so soft but so tired. He looks older than he ever has, but that's not to say he looks old because he doesn't, he just looks like a man who carries so many burdens. "You didn't say you weren't mine. If you'd have said you were Maddox's she'd have probably started hugging you, not biting you."

"I didn't have an opening."

"You did. You just didn't take it."

I wince. He's right. I had thought about saying that I wasn't even with him but I don't like lying, I've done enough of that in my lifetime. I figured just not saying anything would be better. "I'll deny it if anyone asks... unless you want to tell Maddox?"

He blows out a breath. "You've also been thinking about it?"

"I'm just worried he'll find out before we get to tell him ourselves."

He presses his groin into me. "Let's not talk about this now."

I reach between us for his belt and undo it quickly as he tugs my shorts down to my knees and I manage to wriggle one foot free.

He doesn't wait, the second I palm him with my hand he nudges inside, filling me completely. I sigh happily, never feeling more aroused than when I'm with him.

His lips touch mine gently as he slowly glides in and out. Pushing himself to the hilt and withdrawing to the tip so slowly it's all I can do to stop myself from mounting him and riding him in a way I know he loves.

Unfortunately, despite the fact I'm enjoying every second, a greater reasoning falls over me when I realize what's happening.

"You forgot to suit up," I whisper in his ear as his breathing quickens in mine.

"I know," he murmurs. "I'll pull out."

"That doesn't exactly work." I smile, shivering when he jabs his cock into me to get me to be quiet.

He hooks my leg over his arm and circles his hips, pressing the base of his throbbing cock against my clit. I'm going to lose it soon, I can feel myself spiraling. It's so good. It always is with him but this is different.

I orgasm, gripping his body with my limbs and my sex and he joins me, thrusting inside despite the fact he said he'd pull out.

It's okay, I tell myself, the chances of me getting pregnant are really slim. It's rare that it happens in a month. It takes years for some people. We'll be fine.

"I know I always said I'd never ask you for anything," I whisper against his neck, swallowing my pride as his body twitches on mine and in mine.

"Go on," he says gruffly, leaning up so he can see my face in the dark. The sun set sometime during the police interrogation.

"Can you please replace the underwear you've ruined?"

"Done," he replies easily, kissing me again.

When he climbs off my body I feel cold. He walks away, leaving me alone to my thoughts and I watch him ascend the wide staircase that leads to his room.

That's it?

I had thought for a moment there that he might actually stay with me for longer than a minute after finishing. How foolish am I?

For a moment there I thought he might have come to care for me. Does that mean I've come to care for him?

Shit.

What am I doing here?

Sargent

"She's fine," I say to my son on the phone. "Your mother isn't. She's probably going to jail and I'm not dropping the charges this time, not even for you and if you ask Tempest to I'll kick your ass myself."

"No, she can't keep doing this," Maddox replies, sighing heavily. Why couldn't I have given him a better mother? "What happened to rehab?"

"Who knows? I haven't heard from her since before you left for your travels."

"Throw the book at her." Maddox has never said such a thing about his mother. He has always defended her because of his unconditional love for her, and the shit she has done to him still makes my blood boil. "Are you sure, Pest is okay?"

"She's fine, she's sleeping."

He clears his throat and exhales sharply. "I saw Mom last week."

I've always tried to protect him from his mother, even when he was little and we all lived together. She never had the patience to be a mother. One could say she was lacking that maternal instinct required. Saying that, when he got old enough, I never stopped him from finding her, until the last few times she broke into our home and stole our things under the guise of motherhood.

Last I heard of her was a few months before he left when he said goodbye and she seemed to be genuinely doing well.

I fucking hate her.

She's the type of person that should never have money. She couldn't handle it when our income became disposable.

After that abusive relationship ended I promised myself I'd never get into another one again. Seeing the way it affected my son as he grew was enough to put me off ever trusting another person with my child.

"On purpose or...?"

"I called her to see how she was doing, I left a voicemail but she didn't answer, so I went to her old place." He bites on his lip looking nervous and uncomfortable. "She wasn't there, they told me where she'd be. She looked good, Dad. She was staying with a friend, I saw the apartment, it was nice. She needed a deposit to get her own place..."

I close my eyes and turn away from him.

"I'm sorry."

"Shit." I turn back to him and shake my head. "Don't ever apologize for trying to help your mother."

"I'm the reason..."

I slam my hand on the table and demand, "And don't ever, I mean *ever*, blame yourself for your mother and her demons. Her choices are her own."

He nods but still looks sad. "I can't believe she attacked Pest."

"And Devon."

"He probably deserved it."

I chuckle because he's right, he probably did. I should send him a text to see how he is. I pull my phone out to do just that, cringing when he reminds me about the commitment we have tonight.

"Morning." Tempest enters the kitchen looking no worse for wear.

I smile at the sight of her before I can stop myself and Maddox, seeing my reaction, smiles too. He moves to her and envelops her in a tight embrace, resting his chin on the top of her head. His eyes meet mine as they sway from foot to foot and he whispers his apologies into her hair.

When she pulls back, he gently touches the bite mark and frowns, shaking his head.

"I'm sorry," he whispers and I can't look away from their private moment. I can't look away as she reassures him it isn't his fault and his eyes soften. He looks devastated that she's hurt and I'm panicking inside. Is he in love with her and just doesn't know it yet?

"I have people coming over tonight," I say, breaking up their intimate moment. "Devon and a few acquaintances. Poker night."

"Poker night?" Maddox looks intrigued but I nip it in the bud.

"Not for you, Son, as much as I enjoy your company this is a meeting I have to focus on."

"Anything interesting?" Tempest smiles kindly at me.

I nod and reply, "Trying to break out of a contract. It's unlikely but if I can get him to make the bet and I win..."

"What contract?" Maddox looks equal parts curious and nervous. "Anything I can help with?"

"No." I look at Tempest and contemplate telling her about the setup in the yard.

I've been thinking about it nonstop, hoping she'll stumble upon it but I'm also terrified she and Maddox will read into it.

"There's something for you in the yard, by the barrier wall," I say, looking at my phone.

"What?" Maddox asks, looking excited.

"Not for you," I reply and his eyebrows hit his hairline and Tempest's lips part with surprise. "For her."

"What?" Maddox repeats but his tone is darker this time.

I walk away, taking the stairs three at a time as they race each other to the garden.

I move into my bedroom but because of the gazebo I can't see her reaction. I can see Maddox's though as he slowly makes his way to the area she beat him to and then, at the edge of the roof, he stops and looks up at me.

His eyes curious, his mouth flat. Until she grabs his arm, squealing with glee, and yanks him out of my sight.

I should have thought about the roof getting in the way of my view of her.

Fuck. I didn't want the sun to burn her as she painted. Maddox said she could stand at an easel for hours at a time and not even realize it.

At least she sounds happy.

11

Tempest

All day I've been aching at work to go home and paint but by the time I've finished, the sun is setting and Devon is dressed in a tailored suit, ready for the evening of poker.

"You look dapper." I grin at him as he walks me to his car.

"You look sweaty."

"Thanks," I reply, rolling my eyes but I haven't lost my smile. "I hope you win."

"If I win, I'll take you to that new dessert shop you and Fidget were squawking about all day today to anyone who will listen," he promises.

Fidget is another really sweet woman who works for him, she's obsessed with anything chocolate and anything cake. I'm more obsessed with ice cream but I'm extremely careful when I eat it; I get the worst brain freeze and the biggest thighs. I don't know her real name, just that everybody calls her Fidget because she can't sit still. She's the only person exempt from working at the checkout for this very reason.

"Heck, seeing you smile like that, I'll take you anyway." He chuckles and I don't know what to say so I don't say anything.

He turns on the radio and we begin the journey home.

As promised, when we get there, I go straight to my room and frown when I see paper bags, from a multitude of stores sitting on the bed.

There's a note propped up against them which I unfold carefully and read:

"Dad's personal shopper picked out a few things for you.
Anything you don't like/doesn't fit we can return.
X
Mad"

Maddox bought me new clothes?

He said he would but I had assumed we'd go to a local bargain store and I'd dig through their messy racks until I found something wearable. The clothing in these bags cost more than I could earn in a year.

I'm equal parts annoyed and happy. I try to push the annoyance down but I don't want to feel indebted to him more than I am already. It's bad enough his father just bought me all of those expensive paints and pencils and books and canvases...

Now this?

I feel like such a charity case.

Tempest: Thank you for the clothes but they're too much. We have to take them back and we'll go to Target or something...

Maddox: My dad insisted. The washing machine turned half of your shit pink. Take it while he's in a good mood and then hock them for spending money when we go to England.

I laugh at that and shake my head as I dare to peek into bag number one. I can't help but squeal as a flutter of excitement crashed through my veins as I pull out a gorgeous, gray, lace summer dress. I try it on and when I know it fits, I hang it up in my closet and move on.

The next bag has more summer outfits, denim shorts, waist high and hip huggers, T-Shirts, vests, all things I already wear, just fancier versions. He hasn't tried to change my look. He's only given me a variety and I love that.

Except the last few boxes and bags which are full of at least five different sets of underwear.

I dive into the shower and scrub my body before daring to don a black, lace, satin thong-bra-stockings set with matching suspenders that sits on the waist.

I stare at myself in the mirror, biting my lip as I take in my appearance.

I feel incredible. It fits so well and looks amazing. I've never had a bra that fits better than this. I don't ever want to take it off.

When I turn off the light so I can take a selfie in the mirror, with only the moonlight highlighting my figure, I see an odd shape at the edge of my humongous window.

When I narrow my eyes to get a better look, a flash of teeth smile at me and dark eyes drag over my image. He lifts something that glints in the moonlight and taps it against the glass.

Still staring at the knife-wielding shadow, I scream and

move to the door but it flies open and I collide with a strong chest.

Sargent holds me against him as somebody else enters my bedroom with a gun drawn.

"There's a man!" I panic, pointing at the window where the shadow was. "He had a knife, he was standing right there, just looking at me."

"Dev," Sargent yells, "get my gun, search the area."

"On it," I hear him call from the distance.

As my panic subsides I remember my state of undress and feel eyes on me belonging to the man who entered my bedroom with his gun drawn. He's tall and I wonder what's in the water around here to make men this big. He's muscly, humongous, even. He has tattoos from his jaw down and I can see the shape of one under his eye but I can't make it out in the dark.

Sargent wraps me in the blanket from my bed, covering my body.

"Avert your eyes, Stone," Sargent snarls at him. "Everybody get the fuck out."

The man in question nods his handsome head but touches my shoulder with a finger as he passes, dragging it over the bare skin.

"Stone," Sargent warns and I watch the man tuck his gun into the back of his jeans and tug down on the bottom of his leather cut. It has an emblem on it, a twisted skull of some kind of animal and the words, "*Soulless Jackal*" printed around it.

He's a biker. I've never met a biker before but I've seen enough on TV to know to be wary.

HIS FATHER

"Are you alright?" Sargent asks, gripping my shoulders and looking me up and down.

I nod. "I am so sorry for bothering you. I just freaked. I was trying on the clothes and the light was on so I don't even know how long he was there for. What if he got pictures?"

"It's okay," he assures me, setting me on the bed and kicking an empty bag out of the way. "Did you see what he looked like?"

I shake my head. "Not exactly. I mean..." I rack my brain, seeing him standing there... "I was too busy focusing on the knife. It was huge. He kept tapping it against the window like he wanted me to see him."

I wrap my arms around his waist, standing again, and press my face into his shoulder.

"It's okay," he whispers, kissing my hairline. "You're safe."

My adrenaline slowly subsides but only to a less erratic level.

I reach up, hook him around the back of his neck and push my lips onto his.

He seems taken aback for a moment, but then, as the blanket drops, he grips my rear with both hands and pulls me toward him. I feel him grow against my hip as his tongue dips into my mouth, tasting me.

Turning, he pushes me against the closed door and hooks my leg over his arm, moaning when his length pushes against my tingling mound.

"We don't have time," he breathes, pulling back and cupping my jaw with his large hand. "I've got a poker game to win." His lips trail down my neck. "You have no idea how sexy you look right now." His fingertip trails over the seam of my bra. "Keep this on and I'll sneak in later."

"What about that man?" I ask, looking at the window again but seeing nobody there.

"Don't worry, whoever he is has likely been frightened off. If you're scared, get dressed and go up to my room." He runs his thumb over my lower lip. "I'll try to get this over and done with as quickly as I can."

I nod and pull away from him, grab the gray dress and slip it over my head, then I follow him barefoot to the dining area where three men are standing with the doors wide open. Devon returns and shakes his head at Sargent who sighs.

"Footprints but no sign of him."

"He won't be back," Stone assures us, glancing at me. When he catches me looking, he winks and Sargent pulls me behind him as he steps forwards. "Not while we're here."

I move to the stairs, keeping my head down, when Stone's hand reaches out and he grabs my bicep.

"Are you not going to introduce us?" he asks Sargent as he looks at me with curious eyes. His long, dark beard surrounds curving lips and surprisingly nice teeth. There's a curiosity in his eyes that makes me feel as naked as I was when he burst into my room.

"No," Sargent replies and Stone's hand tightens on my arm, only slightly, it doesn't hurt but it does tell me I'm not going to be able to escape.

"Perhaps she'll introduce herself?" He grins, raising a dark brow.

I wet my lips and his eyes move there. "I'm Tempest."

"Tempest?" He tests my name and his grin broadens. "I like that, a name fit for a biker, or an old lady."

"Stone," Sargent warns and Stone chuckles but still doesn't release me. The other men watch on, interested by the exchange. They're all wearing the same cut as Stone, all but one. Devon shifts on the spot by the open doors, he looks as uncomfortable as I feel.

"And why are you here, Tempest?"

"I'm visiting, from England."

"That explains the accent, though I had thought you were Australian for a minute there." He chuckles and nods to Sargent. "You his?"

"Sorry?"

He gives my bicep a little shake. "I said, are you his?"

"No," I reply quickly.

His smile broadens. "You his son's?"

"I'm just a friend of the family."

"She's mine," Sargent snaps, yanking me backwards and into his chest. I slam against him with an oomph.

"She doesn't seem to think so." He raises a challenging brow. "You fucked him? Bet you're a good fuck. You got that look about you. Raise hell with a body like yours."

"Stone," the man in the suit warns. "Perhaps pissing off Mr. Wolf is not in the best interests of the club at this point."

"I'm just playin'!" Stone declares to the room and moves away. "Speaking of playing, have you ever watched a live match of poker?"

"I've had enough excitement..."

"Sit your sweet ass down and watch me take your man's money."

Sargent curses under his breath and everybody returns to the table where a fresh deck of cards is shuffled, cut, shuffled, cut, and then dealt.

I sit quietly as one of the men brings us drinks, myself included. I'm forced to take a shot of whiskey for my nerves and Sargent keeps one hand on my thigh at all times. He wins a few hands, loses a few, but it isn't until Devon, the suit guy who I know now to be called Banks, and the last guy in a leather cut who isn't serving drinks, are out, that things get tense and Sargent releases me.

At this point it's no longer a game of skill but a game of luck and stupidity.

Their piles of chips shift in height as they both win and lose. That is until finally, after another hour and a few more drinks giving them both a buzz, Sargent leans back and speaks.

"This is getting boring."

"I agree," Stone replies, winking at me. "You wanna make it more interestin'?"

"Depends what you want," Sargent places his hand back on my thigh.

"Depends on what you want."

His warm hand stiffens, gripping my thigh with near pain as he looks at his cards again. "I want out of our contract."

Stone's eyes turn... well... stony. "Scuse me?"

What sort of contract does he have with this kind of person? Stone oozes danger. He terrifies me.

"I lose, you get a bigger percentage," Sargent continues, shrugging and downing the rest of his drink.

Devon eyes them both warily. I just want to be anywhere but here.

Stone grins, showing a slither of teeth beyond his parted lips. He too leans back and looks at me. "I'll accept your deal, but you'll have to sweeten it." His eyes drag over me again, his tongue runs over his lip, making it shine in the soft light coming from the kitchen area. "If I win, I get thirty percent of your company, and a night with your girl." The room stills and Sargent's hand grips my thigh so hard it hurts.

My stomach is in knots. I feel sick. He can't be serious?

"That's only a ten percent increase, I'm being generous," Stone adds, looking at me again.

"You can't be fucking serious?" Devon laughs humorlessly, standing quickly. "We don't trade women, especially unwilling women."

"Only need a few seconds to work my magic and she'll be as willing as a bitch in heat."

I look at Sargent who has yet to talk. He's staring at Stone, a vacant look in his eye.

"Are you considering it?" I hiss, pulling away so sharply I nearly fall from my chair.

"Just one night, can't promise she won't leave you for me though." Stone winks at me as I look back and forth between them.

"I don't want to sleep with you."

He looks unphased by my words and simply stares down Sargent. "You called this for your freedom, didn't you?"

"This game is over," Sargent declares, standing and pulling me up beside him.

My body deflates, the fear leaving me as he pulls me into his side and kisses my hairline.

"Aww, man, I was just twisting your dick." Stone grins, leaning back but his eyes linger on me. "Don't end the game."

"I think it's prudent at this point." Sargent's arm remains firmly around my shoulders. "I need to look into who the fuck was in my yard looking at my woman in her room."

Stone's eyes become stony again. "I hear that. You need any help dealing with the creep you just let me know."

Sargent nods his thanks and looks at Devon. "See them out, I need to check over the surveillance." I look up at his profile and smile at him shakily. My body is still humming from the adrenaline of the night but even more from the fact he just ended the game for me. I know, from his earlier tone, how important this was to him, I hope he gets another chance to make the changes he needs.

"You figure out who it is, just call," Stone insists, shaking Sargent's hand and winking at me. "We'll make sure he doesn't bother you again. You know you got our protection, Wolf. Use it."

Sargent leads me to the stairs.

I let him guide me to his room which when I enter, I take in like it's the first time seeing it. I've been in here a few times but I can't help appreciate it with each visit. The dark wall on the left, the windows overlooking Malibu and the yard, the four-poster king bed with dark blue bedding and rather fluffy white pillows. It's a nice room. A really nice room.

The rug is still in the corner of the two walls of glass that the bed rests opposite. I bite my lip at the sight of it. We haven't touched it since the day of the photos. I imagine it still smells like the sweet, strawberry body oil.

"Are you alright?" he asks me softly when I stop in the space between his bed and the door. His fingers dig into my shoulders and arms, sliding up and down. It feels nice and helps alleviate some of the stress I feel. I'm not sure anything has kicked in yet. My mind keeps replaying the man at the window with the knife, then fast-forwarding to the moment Stone decided to enter me into the wager.

"I thought you were considering his offer," I whisper, recalling Sargent's face

He kisses my neck, which feels so good, and wraps his arms around my waist as we stare across the dark room together. I shiver in his embrace, always ready and willing to be touched by him. "Never."

"You told him I'm yours."

"You are," he murmurs, trailing the tip of his nose along the edge of my hair. "I'd never hurt you."

His words stop my breathing. "Don't say things that will make me feel more for you than I should."

He walks me to the rug and doesn't stop until my bare toes are wriggling in the super soft faux fur. When his fingers find the hem of my dress and lift, I raise my arms and wet my lips.

"We're just sex," I say quietly. "We're just doing this. No complications."

His hand holds mine above my head as he circles me and then dips his lips to kiss my throat. After hooking my arms around his neck, large, warm hands finally drift over my curves before palming my breasts through the black lace.

"You are the most beautiful woman I have ever laid eyes on."

His words and following kiss make everything else melt away for a while. He normally has me on my back by now but he seems content to just taste me and I'm okay with that. I like kissing him. More than I should.

"Get in bed," he whispers after another moment. "I have to deal with Devon, check the surveillance and lock up. In no particular order."

I'm about to protest when he lifts me into his arms and strides to his bed. He lays me on it and looks at me with so much longing.

"I'll be back soon."

"Maddox will be home soon," I remind him, talking about the fact I'm in his bed and not my own.

"I know," he replies, kisses me again as I pull the blanket over my body, still donning my underwear. I'll get changed into one of his tops after he's gone. "I won't be long."

Does that mean he's actually going to sleep with me?

I don't know how I feel about that. Normally he fucks me and goes away or escorts me back to my own room, or essentially kicks me out. Hence the fact when we do screw, it's usually in my room because it complicates things less. This is whole new territory.

Sargent

I watch the man stand at her window, the cameras around the house caught him trying the back door, but getting spooked and running around the side of the house as a way to escape, only to find her in her room, likely trying on her new belongings as she said she was doing before she saw him.

He tugs on his dick, his movements fast and almost angry as his other hand grips the knife. It looks like a standard knife that we use to chop things up in a kitchen. This terrifies me even more because what the fuck is he going to do with it? Why was he trying to get into my house? Who is he looking for? Was it her all along? Does he know her? It's hard to tell who it is due to his hood being up but I have a couple of half-decent stills of his face. I'm going to edit them for a clearer look.

I've sent a few through to Stone, and some to Devon who left twenty minutes ago, and some to Tucker, my company's head of security.

There's little else I can do but wait to see if they recognize him. I plan on showing some of the edited stills to Tempest but I don't plan on telling her about the fact he has masturbated to her through the glass. It makes me sick knowing he stood there for over an hour watching her, twisting that knife in his hand.

Until we catch this fool we can't let her out of our sight.

I have never known fear like the fear I felt when I heard her scream. It had us all tossing up our cards and racing to her room. Stone had his gun out before he was even out of his chair.

I've never heard a scream of fear like that before.

I'm still feeling the adrenaline from it.

The house is locked up and safe, my son is on his way home but I don't plan on keeping her out of my sight tonight. He can discover us and question me all he likes, tonight I just need to keep her close and keep her safe.

On that note, I shut down my computer and join her in bed. She's rid her delectable body of the underwear that we all unfortunately saw her in and is wearing one of my T-shirts and a pair of my boxer briefs. She still looks ridiculously sexy.

I climb in behind her and lie on my back, looking up at the ceiling, fighting the urge to wrap my body around hers. This is getting complicated.

I double-check on the pistol in my bedside table, it's loaded, the safety is on, it's there for when I need it. I mean *if* I need it which I hope I never will.

Sighing, I rub my hand over my face and glance at the sleeping woman beside me again.

Why did it have to be her? Why can't I be with anybody but her right now? Feeling the way I feel...

I don't even know what I feel, but I know that it's more than I should and definitely not just sex anymore.

"Stop," she murmurs, tensing in her sleep. "Please, just stop."

"Tempest," I whisper, placing my hand on her stomach.

She curls into me immediately and sighs. Her hand rests on my chest and her thigh shifts over mine. I adjust my arm under her neck and relax. This is not something I do but I'll allow it because it feels really fucking nice. She feels really fucking nice.

She smells of berries too, which is also really fucking nice.

I drift to sleep and I don't even feel it.

Warmth surrounds my cock.

So much warmth and wetness.

My eyes blink open, it's still dark but I feel her hands digging into my chest, I feel her bucking against me, slowly at first but faster when she sees me open my eyes.

"What a way to wake up," I groan as my balls begin to burn and tingle and my cock gets harder and thicker inside of her.

She moans, leaning forward and pressing her forehead to mine as her hips circle and move.

"Do that thing you do," she breathes, squeezing her eyes shut.

"That thing?" I question, gritting my teeth because I'm so sensitive I might only last another minute if I don't focus.

"With your thumb," she snaps, sounding angry at me for not immediately knowing what the fuck she's talking about.

"As you wish." I grin in the dark, sliding my hands up her thighs as she continues to bounce on me, sitting upright again. My thumb finds her clit and rolls over it, softly at first but then quicker as she gets wetter.

She mewls and gasps and I know I'm doing it just right. It doesn't help me much though because she's squeezing my dick like never before.

"Your pussy feels like a fucking clamp," I laugh, grabbing her hip with my free hand and forcing her to slow down a bit.

She growls at me and glares too as her hand grabs mine and brings it to her breast. Oh, I like this version of Tempest. She's bossy, and needy. An excellent combination in the bedroom.

"That's it," I tell her, smiling smugly as she grinds on my cock and I play with her sensitive clit. "Get angry, fuck me."

"Yes," she murmurs through her moans and her eyes close. She's losing it. Thank fuck. I've been struggling to hold on for a while now. I want to roll her over and power into her until I find my release but seeing her so wild, free, and unashamed has to be the sexiest thing I've witnessed in my entire life. "Sargent..."

"That's it... say my name, baby. Remember whose cock it is you're fucking."

She stops and gives me a look. "You serious right now?"

I laugh and roll her onto her back before kissing her lips, still shaking with laughter.

She joins in the amusement until I slowly roll my hips back and sharply thrust forward.

I groan when she comes, the walls of her sex flutter, quiver, and pulse around me, making me join her. Why have I never felt like this before her? Why has sex never been this good? With or without a condom it's incredible with her.

She's stunning, the most beautiful woman I've ever seen. I wish I was joking.

I collapse on top of her and fall asleep before my head hits the pillow.

When I wake up again, she's still fast asleep beside me and unfortunately, somebody is standing at the end of our bed. At first, I panic, ready to reach for my gun, but then I see who it is, and mutter a curse under my breath.

"Maddox..."

He looks at me with so much hatred in his eyes. I never wanted him to look at me like that.

"Aren't you going to tell me it's not what it looks like?" he grits, his hands fisted by his sides.

Tempest stirs, I feel her shift on my chest.

I roll out from under her, startling her.

"I was going to talk to you," I say honestly because I was. I'd decided to tell him, with or without her permission because I plan on taking her out on my arm. I plan on making it known that she's mine because I'm not ready to let her go yet. Even as fucked up as this is, I just need a bit more time with her. "I'm sorry you had to find out this way."

"Maddox." She sits upright, her eyes wide as she grips the blanket to her chest and I yank up my boxers that she tugged down last night.

"Him?" Maddox asks her, his face crumpled with disgust. "My dad, Tempest? Really? You're fucking him?"

She stares at him, wide-eyed and frightened.

"Son..."

"Don't fucking call me son. I told you to stay away from her!"

I pass her the T-shirt she was wearing when I crawled into bed with her and she immediately yanks it on.

"Let's talk about this downstairs, over coffee..." I try, reaching for my son but he shoves me away with the strength of a man and I go back a step.

"Fuck you," he hisses.

"Mad..." Tempest whispers, her eyes swimming with tears as she climbs out of bed and reaches for his arm. He shakes her off, gently in comparison to how he handled me.

"Mad, please," she begs, chasing after him.

Tempest

I've never seen him like this and it is killing me. He has to listen. He has to understand.

"Mad!" I cry, following him down the stairs. "Please, *please*, let me explain."

"Explain?" He spins to face me, his cheeks red from anger and frustration. "Explain how you're fucking my dad? *My dad!*" His hand rips through my hair. "He's twice your age. He's a dog. You know this. You said... I never even... How did this fucking happen, Pest? How?"

"I don't know," I admit.

"It's my fault," Sargent tries but it only succeeds in making Maddox worse.

"You back the fuck off. You're vile. She is half your age! You can't give her anything. You've already done everything!" He looks at me now, confusion and rage darkening his aura. He's so angry and hurt. His eyes are projecting so much anger, heat, and confusion it's going to break me. "It's just sex, right? Meaning-less, pointless sex between adults, right?"

He wants me to tell him I can end it at any moment, like right now but I can't find the words. I think about ending it and it hurts. I don't want to end it. Not even for Maddox, but I will if he asks. He's my best friend. So badly I want to say yes. I want to tell him that I feel nothing but lust for the man at my back, but it'd be a lie. He shakes his head and looks incredulous when I don't respond.

"You've fallen for his bullshit." He laughs angrily. "You've actually fallen for him." His eyes narrow on his father. "I told you she puts her heart into things. She's different. I said that. I fucking said that."

"Maddox." I hold onto the bottom of the top I'm wearing for support because I don't know what to do with my hands. "It's not a big deal. I know what I'm getting myself into."

"You don't get it."

"I do."

"You really fucking don't, Tempest," he spits, looking away from me as though he can't stand to look at me.

I grab his shirt with both hands to stop him from walking away. "I know he's your dad and it's probably weird but..."

"Probably weird?" He looks at me now as though I'm crazy which I probably am. "He's my dad. He's the biggest whore I know and you're a fucking idiot if you have feelings for him because he doesn't return them. He drove my mom to drugs and he'll fuck you up just the same."

"Mad..." I breathe but he pushes away and exits the house, slamming the door behind him.

I don't move until I hear his car peel away, tires screeching, engine revving.

"He'll come around." Sargent presses his chest to my back.

I stare at the door a moment longer before I let Sargent pull me away, set me on the bar which is cold against my butt, and make me breakfast which consists of poached eggs and toast.

It tastes amazing but after all of the excitement I don't have much of an appetite.

"I have work soon," I say softly, mostly to break the silence. "Would you mind giving me a lift?"

"A lift," he mimics my accent, or close to it, and smiles softly at me.

He parts my knees and slides me to the edge of the counter where I'm still perched. Then he brings my lips down to his in a deep kiss and hums with it. For a moment I let myself fall under his hypnotizing kiss. Then I pull back and wait for his reply.

"Anything you need," he murmurs, then kisses me again.

12

Sargent

She must have called him thirty times on the way to work, she's devastated. I understand. We were stupid but I don't regret it. I don't regret her.

Though what he said, about me driving his mother to drugs cut me deep, straight through my soul. That's a laceration that won't be healing any time soon. I loved his mother, I treasured her; I gave her everything she wanted but not everything she needed. I often wonder if I'd just been a different kind of person would she be what she is now?

I often look at Tempest and admire her beauty, her lips that are constantly tipped up with a smile, until now. There's never been a time that I've seen her looking so distraught. I've done this to her, I've made her feel this way. If I'd stayed away we wouldn't be here now.

"I'm sorry, Tempest," I try saying to her when we pull into her work's parking lot. "He'll come back."

"He's never been so angry at me," she murmurs, pulling her

hand from under mine when I try to comfort her with my touch. "What if he never talks to me again?"

I know he will, he has to. "I'll try and speak to him."

When she reaches for her car door I push open mine and move quickly to ser side.

"Hey." I press her dainty body into the side of the car and touch my lips to hers. "It'll all be okay."

"Will it?"

"It will," I promise her because it has to be, and I will make it so. "I'll get you after work and we'll go somewhere fun."

Her lifeless eyes spark with intrigue. "What?"

"It's a surprise." I grin, catching her eyes as I cup her cheek. "You down with that?"

"Down with that," she repeats, murmuring, her lips twitch with amusement. "I'm down with that."

"Good." I kiss her again, uncaring if anyone sees, the worst to know now knows. It can't get any worse.

I should end it, I know that would be in everybody's best interests but I'm selfish and I need just a little bit more time.

"Kiss me," I demand because even though she has reciprocated my gentle touches, she hasn't put her passion into it like she usually does. "Kiss me like you mean it."

I try again, pushing my tongue past the seam of her lips and she returns it with fervor, gripping my jacket to keep me close, humming with pleasure as our bodies come together.

"Remember this moment, when you spend the day thinking about whether or not you should leave me," I whisper and silence her with another kiss when she tries to interject. "The worst is over, it doesn't matter if you leave me or not now, it won't change what Maddox knows. So remember this moment. Remember how this feels and remember I'll be there later to get you and whisk you away on some romantic adventure."

She laughs a little but her eyes are still so sad. "Romantic adventure?"

"I'm going to sweep you off your feet," I continue boldly, arrogantly, and calmly.

At that she genuinely laughs and this time it's her that initiates the kiss which I happily return. "It'll be okay."

"It will," I agree. "You'll see."

"I trust you," she says, her eyes connecting with mine. "If no one else, I trust *you*."

"I'll cherish it, nurture it, and..." I kiss her again. "And I'll make sure you never forget."

"Call him," she begs. "Try and make him understand."

I nod and reluctantly step away. "Until later."

"Until later," she replies, jogging to Devon's Shack. Which is nothing like a shack. It's a very modern and expensive building full of top quality sporting equipment.

I don't turn away until she's inside and I don't stop by to see Devon because I can't deal with any more lectures or ill wishes today.

Nothing anybody says is going to make me change my mind. I'm in this now and I'll be damned if anybody pushes me out.

Sargent: It's going to be okay.
Tempest: I believe you.

Then I text my son.

Sargent: Call me when you're ready to talk. Preferably sooner rather than later. We have things to discuss. Not just about Tempest.

As it sends, my disposable phone starts to ring.

"Heads up." It's Stone. I can't be dealing with this today too. "Nastya is in the States, thought I'd warn you. She might drop by. She knows you tried to gamble your way out of the contract. Not sure who told her."

"Fuck," I mutter and rub my face with my hands. "Thanks for the heads-up."

"Don't do anything to piss her off. She's even more crazy since her divorce."

"Noted." I hang up and climb back into my car. This is going to be a tough week.

Maddox: Get fucked...
Maddox: By anybody but her.
Maddox: I fucking hate you.

Definitely a tough week.

Sargent: Neither of us did this to hurt you.
Maddox: It's not my feelings I'm worried about. It's hers! She's the one that's going to get broken when you spit her out.
Sargent: Tell her that, she thinks you hate her.

Maddox: I can't look at her right now. I wish I'd never come back.

I stop messaging him because no good can come of it. He knows where I stand now.

The passenger door opens and Devon climbs into the seat.

When he sees my look, he holds up his hands and says, "Don't worry, I've got Kent looking after her and everybody has seen that fucker's face now that I've put a memo out. He's not getting anywhere near my shack."

"Kent?" I ask, trying to remain passive as a jealous rage surges through me. "As in the big, tattooed security guard that you had to threaten to get him to stop sleeping with your customers?"

He raises a dark brow and flashes his white teeth at me. "You sound jealous."

"I'm not jealous. Why would I be jealous?"

"The same reason you had her pressed up against her bedroom door last night, looking like you were ready to fuck her with everyone in the other room."

I had a feeling he'd seen us.

"I'm not in the mood for lectures," I warn.

"You mean because you're seeing a woman half your age? No judgement. Way I see it, you're only just hitting the same age of maturity that she's at."

I laugh at that because he's right. I am. "I've fucked all this up. She's more trouble than she's worth." The words, though I say them, leave a bad taste in my mouth and I immediately wish I could take them back.

"She's still with you, so clearly you aren't too upset by all the drama."

I shrug. "I always did like to make things interesting."

"So, fill me in. How long you been boning?"

I squeeze the steering wheel and roll down my window as the stench of his strong aftershave dominates the air in the car. "Since the day after our little poolside grilling gathering."

"When *you* lathered her in lotion instead of *me*?"

I roll my eyes. "That would be something you remember." Pause. "Maddox knows. After that shit last night, I convinced her to stay in my room... He came looking for us."

"Oh shit."

"Found us naked in bed together."

"Double shit."

I nod slowly. "Yes, he is not happy."

"Doesn't really surprise me seeing as he's in love with her."

I glare at my old friend. "He's not in love with her."

"He is. Just doesn't realize it yet. Let's get coffee." He rolls down his window and spits out the wad of gum in his mouth. When he smiles at me I put the car in drive and we go but I can't shake what he's just said out of my head. Is he in love with her? Could Dev be right?

Fuck.

"So..."

"What, Dev?"

"Is she as feisty in bed as she looks?"

My lips stretch into a smile and I put away all of my stresses to save them for later. No point worrying about it all now, not until I've spoken to Maddox and know where I stand.

160

HIS FATHER

"Damn," he mutters. "Lucky shit."

"Definitely."

We talk about business and tourism, mundane shit really but shit that helps us get an insight on how we're running things. Even though we're both in totally different lines of work, there's never a time we don't have ideas to bat to each other.

When we go for coffee, Devon flirts with the waitress and pokes fun at me when I don't. His easy banter with her has me thinking to how I was just three weeks ago. It made me feel good to flirt but now, the thought of it makes me feel like I'm betraying the girl I have already. Does this mean we're going steady? I'm getting too old for this shit.

People keep telling me it's time to settle down, but with a woman half my age? Besides, she's passionate about traveling, I doubt I'll be able to make her stay in the same place. Perhaps I could fund it, so she remains faithful to me and returns a few months out of the year?

What am I thinking?

"You look worried," Devon points out, sipping his coffee and placing his phone face down on the table beside it. Mine is in the same position adjacent to his.

"It's just typical that the first woman I enjoy the company of for more than a day at a time, is too young for me, too beautiful, too off-limits."

He nods thoughtfully. "What're you gonna do if Maddox tells you he loves her and asks you to leave her?"

"What I always do when anybody asks me for anything," I mumble and sigh heavily. "Pick the thing that makes me

161

happiest and fuck everyone else. I love Maddox, but he snoozed."

"And he sure losed."

"Not a word."

"It rhymed."

"Don't give up your day job, Jay-Z."

He laughs loudly, drawing the eyes of those around us. "You like her a lot."

"I'm fucking crazy about her, that's what's making all of this so complicated. If she was just sex, I'd wave her off; but I don't think she is. Not anymore."

"You love her?"

"Uh." I shake my head. "Let's not go that far."

"You just said you're crazy about her."

I chuckle but it sounds nervous even to my ears. "In the sense that I can't get enough of her body. She's not like any woman I've ever met. She's calm, sweet, funny... she genuinely cares about shit normal people don't think about. Or normal people I know."

My words remind me of when she was watching TV on the second floor the other day and cried at an advertisement for starving children. She said that's where she wanted to go next. To help them. Seeing those few tears stain her cheeks made me feel things I shouldn't.

This has me panicking about tonight and who she might meet at my surprise. Well, it was my idea but Marcy and Cassius put it all together. The fact they put it together so quickly is astounding. I hope Cassius can make it but if he can't that's good too. He's perfect for Tempest in so many ways.

"Sounds like love to me."

I flip him off and pick up my phone but the screen is blank. "I just need out of this contract and that Russian cunt is coming to make my life hell for a while no doubt."

"Nastya?" he whispers, his brows pulling together.

I nod and bite my lip. "She knows I tried to get out of our deal."

"Fuck. Stone rat you out?"

"He warned me so I doubt it."

"What are you going to do?"

I shrug. "Hope and pray she fucks off without coming to Malibu. I might take an extended vacation until she's gone."

"Not a bad idea."

I finish the last of my coffee and tuck my phone in the inside pocket of my jacket.

"It'll all work out," he assures me. "Focus on your new girl, don't worry about the other shit."

"Oh, I am definitely focusing on her."

He smiles genuinely and mutters, "Lucky bastard."

Tempest

"He didn't call," I say after buckling myself into Sargent's car. "He didn't text, call, send a pigeon..."

"A pigeon?" He smirks, placing his hand on my thigh after putting the car into drive.

"Or an owl."

"An owl," he mimics my accent, so I slap his arm.

"This is serious."

"I know, but not tonight." He turns a corner sharply, still smiling but the creases around his eyes are holding his stress. He might be smiling but I can see he too is suffering. "Tonight, it's about me and you and nobody else."

"You're not breaking this off to save face with your son?"

"No."

I'm surprised by this, I've worried all day. "I thought this was going to be a breakup night."

"That's what you want?"

Is it? I don't know what to think about any of it because Maddox hasn't spoken to me yet.

"Tempest," he snaps, drawing my eyes back to his profile. His smile has gone and the handsome creases around his deep-set eyes are more prominent. "If you're going to end this with me then do so now."

"Maddox..."

"Don't blame it on my son either. Choose what makes you happy."

"His happiness makes me happy," I admit. "He's the only family I have."

"You have me," he says quickly, still looking ahead at the road, glancing at me for only a split second.

"Come on, Sarge," I laugh but there's little to no humor in my tone. "I have you until you tire of me, which won't take much longer if rumors are true about your attention span."

He doesn't deny it but he does add after a pause, "I promise I won't abandon you."

"I'm not your responsibility."

"You're not Maddox's either."

He has a point.

Sighing grievously, I look out of the window and purse my lips for a moment. Finding the right words in a situation as sticky as this and a conversation that's teetering on the edge of argument is hard. "I'm sorry all of this is happening. I wish it wasn't."

"I don't wish that."

At least he knows what to say, this time at least. His words make me smile.

"I'm not breaking this off. I'm enjoying whatever this is and like you said this morning, Maddox knows so there's no use ending it. I'll always wonder if I do."

"Good," he says as his hand comes back to my thigh and squeezes before drifting up to my sensitive spot.

I shiver and return the favor, groping him over her trousers while smiling a mischievous smile. "Why don't we find some-where quiet and just fuck this day away?"

"No." He withdraws his hand from between my thighs and grips mine. "I've made plans for us. Plans that can't be changed. Plans I've spent a lot of time figuring out."

"I am intrigued."

We arrive at a large house, even larger than Sargent's but less glass windows and more walls. It's stunning. The driveway is huge but there are only half a dozen cars parked along the sides.

We pull up at the very end, closest to the exit and I suddenly feel very underdressed when we approach a group of sophisticated-looking adults at the entrance doors.

"Wolf!" an older man calls, and everybody moves to greet us. "It's an honor to have you in attendance and your stunning lady friend, Tempest is it?"

I nod. "I'm at a disadvantage."

"Of course, you are," he chuckles, shaking his head as I look around the crowd of beautifully, expensively dressed individuals. I look a mess but I've just finished a long shift. "I'm Maxwell. This is Jenny, Debra, Hamish, Louis, and Josh."

"Hi." I give them all a little wave and they politely do the same.

"Come," Sargent urges, his hand on the small of my back as he leads me into the magnificent house and straight through to the garden where a large stage has been set up with comfortable-looking chairs making sections on the soft grass.

"It's a theatre?" I ask, surprised.

What on earth is going on?

There are a few people in the crowd who are part of their own conversations. They wave but keep to themselves as Sargent takes me straight to a man at the side in a hut-like bar. We order popcorn and drinks and Sargent then leads me directly to the front row.

"What are we watching?" I ask him quietly. "Why does that guy have a theatre in his garden?"

"Actually, it's in my garden." A male voice chuckles to our left and Sargent, with a huge grin on his face, stands and greets the man. He's not as tall as Sargent or as handsome in my opinion but I bet he could certainly turn heads.

They hug like old friends and smile at each other.

"I didn't think you'd come." Sargent pulls me into his side. "This is Tempest."

"Tempest." The man's tone is one of surprise, like mine moments ago, and his eyebrows hit his hairline. "It's a pleasure. I'm Cassius, this douche's oldest friend and his son's godfather."

"Oh my God, I've heard so much about you," I tell him, feeling awed as I shake his hand. "I was in your program last year in Surin!"

"I thought your name sounded familiar. Not every day you hear the name Tempest."

"I'm sorry we never got to meet. The weekend you were visiting I was really ill with pneumonia and other ailments."

His smile is sympathetic. "Yes, I recall a few of the crew came down with something."

"It was horrendous but we powered through it. We helped so many people on your money..."

"Lost a few too," he mutters, looking sad.

I place my hand on his arm. "It wasn't in vain. They were remembered and celebrated always."

Sargent clears his throat.

"Sorry, I'm talking your ear off. I'm just... it's great to meet you, Cassius."

"Not at all." The friends share a look and I wonder if Cassius approves of me. It's extremely important to me that he does, not simply because of who he is to Sargent and Maddox, but because of all he has done for the world. "Will you be joining our movement next year? We're tackling Africa next. I'm trying to convince Sargent to donate to the cause."

Sargent clears his throat and shifts against me when I reply,

"I would love to! Have the details been sent over to Benny and his people? They usually keep me updated."

"Benny isn't on this particular tour. If Sargent has your details I will personally email you, how's that? We need as many people as we can get."

I try not to buzz with excitement but it's impossible. "Thank you."

"Isn't the part of Africa you are visiting extremely dangerous?" Sargent puts in, sounding annoyed and worried.

"That's kind of the point of going," I respond, my smile not wavering. "To make life better over there for those who have to live there permanently. Nobody should have to live in fear."

Cassius holds out his fist and we bump knuckles like bros.

"Enjoy the show, I'll catch up with you both afterwards." Cassius winks at me, slaps Sargent's arm and moves on to greet other people. I watch him go and then smile at Sargent who has a brow raised at me.

"Should I get you both a room?" he asks but I see his lips twitch.

"Shut up." I kiss his jaw and look at Cassius once more over my shoulder. I'm still a little bit starstruck. I can't help it.

"You've impressed him."

"I'm an impressive kind of gal, what can I say?"

He pinches my thigh making me squeal, and we sink into the love seat which is just big enough for both of us.

"So, what are we watching?"

I grab a handful of popcorn and stuff it unattractively into my mouth.

Sargent kisses my sweet lips and pulls my legs over his lap. "You shall see."

The lights from around dim and the stage suddenly lights up with a powerful spotlight.

It's the man from the doorway, Maxwell.

He addresses the crowd which has grown in the time we were talking. "Welcome to this impromptu performance, hosted by the gracious and wonderful, Cassius Lepore and organized by the incredible and extremely handsome, Sargent Wolf, and the lovely Marcy."

Extremely handsome indeed.

I look around for Marcy but don't see her.

"She can't stand the play," Sargent explains. He's apparently a mind reader.

I look at him sitting to my right as he draws patterns on my thigh with his fingers.

"You organized this?"

"We do hope you enjoy the screening of The Tempest. A Shakespearean classic if I do say so myself. One of our favorite pieces to perform."

"Oh my God," I whisper, and my fingers fly to my lips.

The spotlight dims to nothing and Maxwell quietly exits the stage.

"Is this a coincidence?" I ask Sargent. "Were you already hosting? Or is this..."

"For you," he admits quietly, smiling gently at me.

Is this because of the conversation I had with him and Devon in the garden that day? Devon asked if I'd ever seen the play, I admitted I hadn't. I didn't even realize Sargent was listening. He had such a bitter look on his face.

"There was nothing within a six-hour drive or flight so I flew the play to you instead."

I push my lips onto his, wishing I could straddle him and fuck him into oblivion, wishing I could worship his body to show my appreciation but the play is beginning.

It's brilliant, even though I can only understand some of what they're saying, the bits I do understand are powerful and will forever remain in my mind. This is incredible. I never want it to end.

We sit silently, eating popcorn until the middle break, where Sargent gets a popcorn refill and more drinks and accosts me with his lips some more.

How did he do any of this?

When the play ends I clap and cheer louder than anyone else there. In true British fashion of course.

The actors and actresses were brilliant, their clothing amazing, the stage props though quickly put together are so cleverly made.

"I want them to do it again," I whisper, wiping tears from under my eyes. "This is the sweetest thing anyone has ever done."

Sargent catches me when I throw myself at him and kiss him hard. The emotions I'm feeling are too much.

"Favorite part?" he asks.

"When she finally declared her love for Ferdinand."

"Ah, of course that would be the bit you choose." He smiles, looking up to the heavens.

"I didn't really understand the rest of it," I whisper in his ear, making him laugh out loud. "But I'll never forget when she declares that she'll weep at her unworthiness to be his." I wet my lips. "That's how I feel with you sometimes... minus the lovey mushy stuff. I just mean because you're you and I'm me."

"What's wrong with *you?*"

I hesitate, shrug and reply, "I have nothing to offer you in return for everything you give to me. I have no family, no friends outside of Maddox that I can rely on, no money or job, no qualifications..."

"You have so many qualities that you didn't list it's almost laughable how insecure you sounded just then," he scoffs, not being mean, he's just not great with words. "You're the most compassionate and kindest person I know. You're so calm."

"That's because I was a Buddhist monk in my past life. According to Facebook."

"You're funny, clever... extremely talented." He pulls me toward the house, away from the crowd and immediately pushes me up against the wall. "Stunningly beautiful. Perhaps even the most beautiful woman I have ever met."

"Coming from a god such as yourself I'll take that as a major compliment."

I relax into his body, returning his kiss but push away his wandering hands. "Not here. People are everywhere."

He smiles in the dark and kisses my shoulder. "Come, I promised Cassius I'd find him after the play. Would you mind if he joined us for dinner? I know I said tonight is for you and me but..."

"Are you kidding? Why even ask? He's come from across the country! I'd be offended if you didn't invite him."

He kisses me again and suddenly dips his hand into the front of my jeans.

I squeal, not expecting it at all but then I melt because he presses his palm against my clit as his finger sinks inside.

"Sargent." I hiss his name but I don't know if it's because I want him to stop or I need him to continue. Both are tangling together on this web of pure lust, adrenaline, and arousal he's brought me to.

My head lolls back as he fucks me with his hand, kissing my neck before watching my reaction as I come undone by his touch alone.

I choke out a cry with my orgasm. His satisfied, smug, aroused grin only powers my climax further. I can't handle it all. It's too much. My legs nearly buckle so I grip his shoulders as he withdraws his hand and then sucks his fingers into his mouth.

Bloody hell.

"I hate you," I breathe, feeling limbless. "Seriously. Why would you do that now?"

"There you are." Cassius appears from out of nowhere. "Come, let's thank them for their performance and be on our way. We have so much to celebrate."

"Did she finally sign the papers?" Sargent asks and Cassius taps the side of his nose.

After spending half an hour chatting and thanking everybody who came, we follow Cassius in his expensive sports car to a restaurant somewhere in LA. I don't follow where we're going because my head is bobbing up and down in Sargent's lap.

I suck his length, making him growl as I swallow as much of him as I can take. It's not something I've done a lot of so I'm not perfect but it sure works for him.

He rips up my head before he finishes and kisses my numb lips.

"We're coming up to traffic," he says, sounding disappointed.

"I wish I'd changed first. I look so out of place again."

"You look beautiful," he assures me, bringing my hand to his lips.

I'm wearing a peach dress and heels but I'm not wearing stockings because I've been working all day. My hair and makeup aren't exactly what I'd call neat after a long day so I remove most of my residual eye makeup and pray that just my mascara and some lip balm is enough.

"Where are we going?"

"His favorite restaurant, it's a Chinese place. Not too fancy so no valet which means we'll have to find parking."

"You sound so horrified by the prospect." I giggle upon seeing his expression. "Snob."

He growls at me playfully and bites the side of my hand.

"I just touched your dick with that."

He throws it away and I laugh uncontrollably as he wipes his tongue on the side of his sleeve.

Sargent

I push in her seat for her, it's ingrained in me to do so. I was raised with the manners of a gentleman in public. Though I simply enjoy seeing her smile when I offer her small gestures like this.

"I did invite Maddox," my oldest friend, who I have known since I was only seven years of age, says softly but with a huge smile. He's likely finding this entire thing amusing. I take the menu he offers and so does Tempest. "But he said to tell you you're a cunt. His words not mine."

I smack my lips. "Sounds right. He's unhappy with me."

"So, you were his girlfriend or...?"

Tempest blanches and shakes her head. "No, nothing like that. We were close, have been for a year but it's never been romantic."

"What about sexual...?"

I kick my friend under the table, he flinches but his smile remains.

"Doesn't that fall under romance?" She's adorably naïve and now I feel like the cunt my son has deemed me to be.

Cassius raises a brow at me, likely thinking the same thing. "You went traveling together?"

She nods but doesn't get to answer as the waitress comes for our drinks order.

Cassius either forgets he asked or just decides he's not interested and moves on the conversation. "Africa, next year..."

Her eyes light up and I can't stop the pang of hatred I have at him for being able to get her to respond that way so easily.

"I've always wanted to go, there are so many causes over there that are so close to my heart." She places her hand over her heart as she speaks. I've never seen her look more beautiful than in this moment with a fiery determination in her eyes and a confidence to her body language that she doesn't usually have.

I wish I brought my camera.

"Why did you get into traveling to impoverished places, or how?" He keeps his eyes on her and I want to kick him again. He likes her and if what he's saying is true, he's divorced now which means he'll be looking for something to fill that gap.

I'd like to say he wouldn't fuck someone who I'm close to but right now I'm not so sure. Perhaps I'm being paranoid.

I did plough his wife once, with his permission and because she asked... We were young and extremely drunk. So perhaps he considers I owe him one.

I'm being ridiculous.

All of this from one conversation that has hardly begun?

"Honestly, I couldn't afford to travel on my own so I joined RGF's campaign. We spent a few months on Turkey's border, taking water to the refugees they wouldn't let through." She's told me a little about this but not much. "I never wanted *fancy* traveling. I mean, it would have been nice but at the time I was already on and off the streets anyway."

She didn't tell me that part of her past.

When she sees my expression, which is likely one of shock and worry, she pats my hand and continues, "It's just one of those things. I figured anywhere was better than there. I made friends who I'll keep for life, but eventually moved onto a different campaign, one where women are held in higher regard."

"They're sexist?"

She shrugs. "They were where I was but their culture is a lot different."

"And eventually you found your way to my campaign?"

Her worried frown becomes a beaming smile. "I did and it was the best ever. We helped so many people and the places we visited were stunning. I met Maddox during one of my rare nights off."

"Can we rewind back to the homeless bit?" I ask firmly, likely putting her on the spot but I need to understand.

Her cheeks pink. How can she be ashamed of such a thing? Life throws us all so many curveballs. Seeing me now, one wouldn't believe it, but I was a paycheck away from homelessness too.

"It was after my dad died. I was too old for foster care but too young to rent anywhere." She clears her throat and the waitress brings our drinks and takes our food order. I'm happy when she orders what she wants and not just what's inexpensive. "But life became pretty great after that. My dad wasn't a good man so nobody missed him, not even me."

"Well there's no pressure on the Africa thing," Cassius says, and I know he struggles to find people for his missions so it's no surprise that he is in fact putting on the pressure.

"I can give you my email and number so you can send over the details? But Africa is one of the places I've really wanted to go anyway..."

"Give it time, think it over," I insist, hating that she can so easily make plans to be away from me for what could be months on end.

Am I thinking that far ahead? She's likely being realistic.

I know she thinks I'll get bored, I do tire easily of the same thing but she's, for lack of being a cliché, *different*.

I have a hunger for her that I'm not sure I'll ever satisfy.

"What a splendid evening. My wife is finally no longer my wife and I may have found somebody for Africa." Cassius beams, holding up his drink and she clinks hers against it.

"You'll be going to this one yourself?" I ask. "How will you find the time?"

"While you've been slumming it with your employees," he jests. "I've found myself a couple of replacements to handle my shit. I'm not getting any younger. It's time to do the shit I want to get done before I get too old. You should consider the same."

Cassius has a point but one I can't linger on for now. There are too many other things to worry about.

13

Tempest

"Maddox is still ignoring me," I tell Fidget. She's the only person I've opened up to about my relationship with Sargent. Not because I'm ashamed... Okay, maybe because I'm a little bit ashamed. "I miss him."

"Give it time."

"It's been nine days now," I grumble, frowning when Kent knocks the cap off a man's head as he walks in the store. "Is there a new no cap policy?" It's the fourth time I've seen him do that today. The customers take it all in stride but still, it's a bit weird.

"Afternoon, boss." Fidget grins at Devon as he walks in with a broken surfboard in two pieces under one arm.

"Take a dive?" I ask, tossing him a towel.

He catches it and dries off his hair. "Something like that. Feel like joining us in the water, Pest?"

Fidget nudges me forward with her hand on my shoulder. "Go on, you've been talking about it nonstop since you started."

"I'm working."

"You'll still be working, you just have to help me keep the kids balanced on their boards." Devon grins, nodding for me to follow. "Go get yourself a company wet suit, they're on the hangers, and meet me in the workshop when you're done. Next class is in half an hour, waves permitting."

"They're wild out there today." Fidget grins, bouncing excitedly. "Go... why are you just standing there?"

I race into the back and grab what I need. The wet suit fits like a body glove. It's so soft and warm. At least he chose a nice and sunny day for me to join in.

When I enter the workshop, I help him wax a couple of boards that have the company logo and colors, sea green and black, and we carry them down to the beach where it is cordoned off for his store specifically.

"Before they get here let's check out your stance." He grins, dropping a board onto the sand with a thud. Surfboards are a lot heavier than they look. "It's easy enough, we have the guides on our boards but everybody has their own way."

"You want me to balance on the board... on the sand?" I laugh and hop on without shame.

"Start on your front, cheater." He smacks my ass then realizes what he just did and we both stare at each other before roaring with laughter. "Please don't sue me, I wasn't thinking... I just did it and immediately regretted it."

"I'm telling Sargent," I jest, dropping onto my front so I'm fully on the board.

It's been a while since I surfed but not so long that I don't remember what to do.

I hop up, using my arms to steady the board and take my stance.

"Not bad but you need to be quicker."

When I lie down for the third time, I squeal as a hard body hits my back.

"This is a rather cushioned board," Sargent chuckles in my ear, kissing my hair and rolling me over. He's wearing his own jet-black wet suit with silver stripes down the arms and legs.

He helps me to my feet and yanks me into his body before kissing me.

"Stop," I snap, slapping his chest. "I'm wearing the company logo. It's against policy."

"She deserves a raise," Sargent tells his friend, ignoring me and grabbing my arse with both hands. "I missed you."

"You did?" I breathe, a mental puddle of goo because of his words. It's the first time he has ever said anything like that but he has been away for two nights with Cassius who is moving back to Malibu for a while to celebrate the divorce from his psychotic ex-wife. They didn't choose very good women to first wed from what I've heard.

He left me in the care of Devon because Maddox still hasn't spoken to either or us and Sargent is worried about my safety. I think the knife-wielding maniac was probably just somebody trying to break in to loot the place, I doubt he'll be back.

"Didn't you?"

I shrug. "Nah, Devon kept me occupied."

"What?" he growls and Devon gives me a look as if to say, "Really?"

I giggle and leap out of the way when Sargent tries to grab me. "I'm working!"

He starts to tickle me and I hate it but also love it. Especially when we fall onto the sand and he kisses me again. His lips and tongue tease mine in a way only he knows how. I hum with appreciation until I remember where I am and what I'm supposed to be doing.

"I'm working," I tell him again, breathlessly, and he touches my cheek with sandy fingers. "I missed you too."

"She did, she's been whining nonstop since you left," Devon chuckles and then puts on a squeaky voice as he says, "What time is it? Is the day over yet? Has he called you? It's been ten minutes since I spoke to him... blah blah..."

I throw a piece of seaweed at him and stick out my tongue when Sargent finally lets me up.

I can't believe he's back. I can't believe how epic it feels that he's back.

"Go on." Devon grins, winking at me. "You're finished for the day. This asshole is taking you surfing."

"Really?" I squeal and throw myself at Devon next. I hug him, covering him in sand and then take the board from the ground. "Come on, old man," I jest at Sargent. "Race you to the line."

"Old man?" He feigns offense. "I'm not the one who always falls asleep first."

"That's me passing out because you're smothering me with your humongous pecks." I laugh, panting as I take off for the ocean.

He follows, cussing me out as we go. We clip our boards to our ankles and dive into the salty, cold, blue sea.

It feels incredible, I wish I'd done this sooner.

We paddle out, racing and ducking under steady waves, he overtakes me but I knew he would and we share a smile when we resurface.

He's so handsome. I've never seen a man more mesmerizingly beautiful. The sun hits his wet profile just right and I wish I had a camera.

We wait, straddling our boards, in the still ocean and I feel the pull of the current beneath my feet. The water rises and we both take off, racing to the edge where we go our separate ways.

He wipes out, not quite making the jump which makes me laugh and lose my balance as I make mine. I fall in sideways and my nose fills with water but I quickly resurface and swim back.

"I beat you already," I shout at Sargent as he swims my way and when he makes it to me, he shoves me off my board, laughing at the top of his lungs. It's okay though because I steal the next wave.

At lunchtime we eat a fruit salad together in his bed because we're both exhausted. It's nice and cozy and it's the first time we've ever just lay together without talking. I remember Devon saying to me just the other night that it's when you get the moments of quiet together that you enter the next stage of your relationship. I'm not sure how true that is but I'm probably going to ruin it.

"I have to tell you something," I say softly, ready to spill my darkest confession to a man who consumes nearly every thought. "It's important and it might change your view of me."

He looks down at me, his eyes nervous but relaxed. "Please don't tell me you fucked Devon."

"What?" I squawk and sit back on my ankles. He shuffles up the bed until his back is against the headboard. "Are you kidding?"

"Sorry, stupid question," he admits, sliding his hand up my thigh.

I scowl at him, pissed off that he'd even ask me such a thing.

"But, it's okay if you did," he carries on and my already nervous heart plummets.

"It's okay if I did?"

He eyes me, scanning me for the truth, as though I'm withholding it from him. At this point I believe the only person holding back is him. "I'd rather know, before I find out from him."

The thought that he might truly mistrust me so much is a nauseating one. The complexity of my feelings for him are too much to bear at this juncture. I'm about to tell him to shove his mistrust up his arse when we hear the door downstairs open and slam shut, all thoughts of conversation leave us both and we race to see who it is.

It can only be one person.

"MADDOX!" I yell, racing down the stairs, past the kitchen and colliding with his chest before he can enter the hall that leads to his room and mine. My arms go around his waist and I hold tight. I daren't let him go because he might not come back again. "You haven't called."

"I'm ready to talk," he tells me and when I look up into his clear blue eyes I see no small amount of troubles swirling around in them.

"Mad..."

"I'm also ready to listen, Pest." When he says my name so softly I smile and hug him for just a moment longer. "I promise."

I want to cry, I didn't realize how much I'd missed him until now. "Don't leave again."

"I won't, but I think you're upsetting my dad, he looks ready to throw you over his shoulder," he whispers and when I peek back at Sargent, he looks away quickly. Alas, I still step away but only a fraction.

"I'm sorry I didn't tell you," I breathe, clinging to the front of his T-shirt with both hands fisting the material.

"I know." He pulls away and looks at his father.

Sargent

"I saw you today on the beach," my son says, crossing his arms over his chest. He looks every bit a man right now. "I saw you making out, I saw you surfing... I saw you leave together." A heavy breath parts his lips and he rubs his face with his hands. "I hate it. I'm not going to pretend to like it. I don't want it rubbed in my face or in front of me at all."

"Duly noted," I reply, fighting the urge to yank her back to my side.

"It's weird. My closest friend, somebody I actually thought I'd probably marry one day..."

I hear her gasp at his words and pray she doesn't fall to his feet to beg for forgiveness. If she leaves me for my son it would be too weird.

"You were supposed to fall in love with me, Pest," he admits to her. "The fact it's my dad... it's weird."

"But we're friends."

He nods his agreement. "We are, while we're young. I sometimes thought... everybody who knew us even said we'd probably end up married one day. Not yet, but one day."

She wipes at her eyes and looks at the floor as I stare at him, waiting for him to get to the point.

"But you're both adults and you've made your choice. I can see that." He leans back against the wall and scratches at the scruff on his chin. "I've never seen you like that with anybody, not even me, not for years at least."

"Like what?" I ask, frowning.

"Like you were with Pest on the beach today. You weren't even like that with Mom." As he says this my heart sinks because perhaps he's right. There's just something about Tempest that makes me feel joyful and expressive. She brings the man I used to know to the surface. "I'm not blaming you or shaming your past. It's just nice to see you happy, even if it is with somebody who is too young for you." He points at Pest. "I don't want to hear about any of it. I'll vomit. Okay? I do not want to know at all."

She nods quickly and moves to hug him again. "Don't leave me again. I missed you."

He returns the hug and glares at me over her head. "I missed you too. But you..." He's addressing me now. "I'm still really fucking mad at you, Dad."

"I know," I reply and even though that saddens me, I'm happy he's home and at least trying to make amends. "It's good to see you."

They separate and the smile she gives me is so bright it could light up the entire sky. It's nice to see her happy again.

"Do you want to do something?" she asks him, following him to his room, completely forgetting about me. "I need to go into town..." The door closes behind them and I want to follow and carry her back to my room. Now that he's back it means I'll have to share her. I've only just come home after two long days away... I don't want to share her yet.

Plus, I'm horny in a way only she can satisfy me. Then again, I'm always horny in a way only she can satisfy me.

14

Tempest

I discover as we're walking through the streets of LA, having decided to go here instead of Malibu, that it's Sargent's birthday soon. In precisely four days.

Maddox told me while we were discussing things, window shopping. I can see that it makes him uncomfortable so I'll not approach the subject at all. Though I kind of want to discuss the whole "marriage when older" thing because I felt a bit blind-sided by that. I also feel awful.

I'm not going to talk about it. It'll just open an awkward conversation that neither of us will enjoy.

Maddox looks good, tanned and clean. His hair is lighter which means he has spent a lot of time in the sun.

"So where have you been?" I ask him carefully, not wanting to trigger any kind of ill feelings.

He smiles in reply. "Just at an old friend's place along the beach. I was jogging when I came across you. I was going to approach you but then Dad appeared." I don't say anything because I promised him I wouldn't. "You're falling for him, aren't you? Not surprising if he's like that with you."

"Like what?"

"Happy and playful, smiling like somebody half his age..."

I snort. "You like pointing out the age gap don't you?"

"Yep, just like you will in a few years when you want kids and a marriage and he's fucking a different woman every weekend because he's bored but he feels indebted to you because you made him feel shit he hasn't felt before and because you're my closest friend. It's such a fucking TV drama."

"Wow, Maddox, say what you really feel..."

"I'm not trying to be an ass. I'm your friend so I'm being real. I don't want you to get hurt but he will hurt you," he states, taking my arm and pulling me into a trinket store. "I need some more incense sticks."

"I need to get high," I murmur, and he hums his agreement. "He can only promise me what every other guy can promise me..."

"No, he can't. Because he can't give you kids or any of that other shit. He won't want babies at his age."

"Maddox, he's not old. He's just older than me."

"That's what he said to Cassius." He runs his fingers over long, narrow boxes until he finds the scent he wants. I love stepping into stores like this, the different flavors in the air combined is so beautiful. "He said you'll leave him soon anyway because he'll never give you what you want."

"You've been talking to Cassius about my relationship?"

He taps me on the head with the narrow box and smiles mischievously. "I've been kept up-to-date with the development of you fucking my dad. I was ready to swoop in and take you away if he fucked you over."

"How chivalrous..."

"I'm here for you when he fucks it up and he will. He can't be faithful. He cheated on my mom, did he tell you that?"

I blink at him. "We haven't approached the subject but I trust him. I'd like it if you didn't put shit in my head that doesn't need to be there."

"And what about the no-kids thing? Doesn't that bother you?"

"No, I'm not sure I want kids anyway and if I ever do I'll cross that bridge when it comes to it. Can't I just enjoy the amazing sex and fun we have without all of this?"

He makes a dramatic puking sound when I say the word sex.

"You brought it up. Which I don't appreciate," I grumble, grabbing the box from him and marching it to the checkout where a woman takes his money and puts the incense sticks into a paper bag.

His phone starts to ring so he steps to the side and I notice a sign on the counter for an herbal, liquid penis enhancer. Like Viagra but you rub it onto the dick, or so it says.

I press my lips together to stop myself from laughing and say to the woman, "Can I get some of that, please?"

She raises a brow at Maddox who looks at me with his jaw on the floor.

"He has performance issues," I add loudly, pointing at Maddox who hangs up the phone as I pay for the liquid and tuck it into my pocket. It's in a little brown bottle with a tiny little cap. Surely this small amount can't be enough. I should have asked for more.

"You're a bitch, you know that?" He shoves me but catches my arm before I stumble and just like that, everything is kind of okay.

Little does he know the gift is for Sargent, as a joke for his birthday. Now, what can I get him as a real present? The man has everything.

Then it hits me. I don't need to buy him something.

I scroll through the images on my phone until I find the one I need. I grin.

"Let's go home, I feel like drawing," I say.

"Drawing what?"

"Never you mind."

"You sounded so British then." He smiles down at me, showing his perfect teeth as he bumps his arm with mine.

I bump him back. "Thank you for giving me another chance, Mad."

"I could say the same to you," he replies, slinging his arm around my shoulder. "Just... don't let me hear it, or see it. Let me pretend you aren't together."

I laugh at that and blow out a breath. "I'm making plans to go to Africa next year with Cassius. He sent me the details last week."

"He said."

"What do you think?"

"I think I want to come with you but I have obligations now. Big ones."

"Why? What's going on?"

His frown returns and his eyes look so troubled. "Nothing to worry about, not yet anyway."

I don't believe him but I don't press. If he wanted to talk about it, he would. So instead of prying, I hug his arm and let him know I'm here if he changes his mind.

~

Sargent

Work has been tough today seeing as I've been neglecting it to spend time with a certain little fiery brunette. I need to do what Cassius has done and hire somebody to handle the mundane shit so I can stay away even more. The business is running smoothly, there are teams of people for all the different areas, but there are some things that are better left to me.

When I'm done, I head to the grocery store and pick up a few things for dinner.

I decide on lamb, I've never made Tempest lamb and if she's already eaten, I'll just make it for myself.

When I arrive home, Maddox is sitting on the sofa, drinking beer and the place stinks of weed.

I sigh and look at his easy smile as he brings a large glass, blue and green striped bong to his lips.

"What is this, a frat house? It stinks in here."

"It was all Pest's idea." He grins and I decide not to chastise him for it. It isn't illegal and it's not like he's choosing this over work. I just wish he'd done it outside. The door is open but I'm still going to get an unwanted secondhand high.

"Where is she?" I ask, looking around the room for her, expecting to find her within the vicinity.

"She's outside painting," he replies and I take off running. "What? What's wrong?"

"Tempest?" I yell, my heart hammering as I round the corner, skidding on the wet tiles from the pool.

"Here," she calls and I find her in her art corner, painting on a large canvas. "STOP!"

I immediately do so and raise a brow when she turns the easel away and picks up a half-smoked joint out of a bowl on the ground.

"What's wrong?" I ask, scanning her with my eyes.

"You're not allowed to see my paintings until they're done. You know that."

"I do know that but are you forgetting about the knife-wielding maniac? You shouldn't be out here alone."

"I have mace spray and a Taser... where did I put them?" She starts looking under sheets of paper and piles of paint trays for the objects. Then she gives up, shrugs and lights the joint.

I'm not a fan of smoking but I have to admit she looks so sexy as she lets it out through her lips, making tiny Os in the smoke.

"Want some?" She holds the joint out to me but I don't take it. "Relax a little, Sarge."

"I don't do that shit and you shouldn't either."

"When I smoke it, I can deep throat," she singsongs, walking toward me, the lit joint still in her hand. She takes one last inhale before dropping it onto the ground.

Her words got my dick hard. Shit. I want to test her theory so badly.

I gasp when she crushes her lips to mine, her eyes still open. Wagging her eyebrows, she breathes out and I breathe in, feeling my throat tighten and tingle as I inhale the smoke from her lungs.

It's only a small amount so it doesn't do much, but it does allow her the opportunity to grip my arms and pull me around the side of the gym, out of sight of my son.

I hardly get the chance to think or protest when she drops to her knees, pulls me free of my clothing and sucks me into her mouth.

"Jees..." I murmur, placing my hand on her head as she goes to fucking town on my cock. Her warm, wet, willing mouth is so soft and perfect. I lean forward and push gently into her mouth. She sucks, licks, grips, and rolls in all of the right places and then she swallows the head of me and I am so glad I came home when I did.

I'm so close, my balls are so fucking tight it's painful. I want to hold out and fuck her right here, but I also want her to swallow me, not just my dick but everything I give her when I come.

"Tempest," I warn, letting her know I'm nearly there. She keeps going, keeps forcing me deeper and deeper, until I cry out. A burn spreads through my body and the most intense orgasm I have ever felt hits me, wave after wave of pure bliss. I force myself to watch her as I shoot into her open mouth and she pumps my cock with her hand, ensuring every last drop is gone before swallowing and hell... I almost come again just watching that.

"God, I fucking love you," I blurt breathlessly and yank her up to me.

She smiles languidly, her lips swollen and red, her hair messy and wild, her eyes relaxed and happy. Then I realize what I said and all I can think is... well shit.

"I love you too," she replies before I can take it back and explain that I meant I love what she does to me, not that I love *love* her. It's far too soon for that... or at least it is for me. "I'm hungry."

She kisses my jaw and starts to walk away.

I just fucked up. I just fucked up so bad.

It's too late now anyway. Even if I do take back what I said, I can't take back what she said and it'll just hurt her if I do. Perhaps one day I'll say it and mean it. I just beg that I haven't given her false hope and tomorrow isn't the day I wake up and decide I'm done. The thought pains me.

Maybe I do love her in my own way?

Whatever I feel, I don't want it to end, not yet.

Tempest

I woke up extra early today to get ready, do my hair and makeup, dress nice and then make him breakfast which I serve to him in bed.

It's just porridge with blueberries because I'm not the best cook in the world and I'm scared I'll mess up anything else.

I place his card and gift on the tray with it and smile as I approach his sleeping form. He's on his back, essentially star fishing beneath the thin blanket in the well air-conditioned room. The muscles of his chest are so defined even as he's lying down you can see the ridges of them.

He told me he loved me. This handsome, incredible, wealthy man loves me. This thought makes my smile become a beam. I can't contain it.

He told me *he loves me.*

Is this what it feels like? Is this what it should feel like? I never want it to end.

"Happy birthday to you," I sing, sitting on the side of the bed as he finally wakes.

His answering smile is so broad and handsome when he sees what I've done. "Porridge?" His accent mimics mine.

"Porridge," I reply and Maddox enters the room without knocking while declaring, "OATMEAL!"

He tosses a wrapped gift onto the bed. "Can't stay, got shit to do. Happy birthday, Dad. Bye, Pest."

"Porridge!" I shout after him when he leaves and Sargent sits up and places the tray over his lap. The legs balance it on either side of his.

"It's been a long time since somebody went to this effort on my birthday." Sargent grins, rubbing his eyes with the palm of his hands. "Maddox used to but not since he was fifteen I think."

He drinks his coffee and waits for me to kiss him.

"So before you open your gift from me, it's not your actual gift. Your actual gift isn't here yet. I'm sorry, I suck I know."

"You certainly do suck," he chuckles, referring to things other than what I'm referring to.

I slap his thigh that's peeking out from under the quilt and then lean forward to kiss it. The soft hair tickles my upper lip as my fingers dig in, massaging his shin. He groans and his head rolls back.

"Open your gifts," I demand, kneeling between his legs so I can rub them both at the same time.

He opens Maddox's first after a few mouthfuls of porridge and he smiles when he sees what it is. I lean to the side so as to get a good look when he hands it to me, still smiling.

I hold the small key chain in my hand and flip it over. On one side is a picture of Maddox holding a baseball bat, on the other is a picture of me. Yes... *me.* Smiling at the camera shyly, my hair blowing across my face. It's a photo he took before we came here. I remember the moment he took it because I was so embarrassed.

"It's a warning," Sargent explains while placing the tray to the side, but I gathered that already. "Remind me to put it on my keys later."

"You want my face on your keys?"

"I want your face near my dick at all times." He chuckles when I scowl at him and starts peeling open the gift from me.

He won't be laughing soon.

"This better not be what I think it is," he murmurs as he reads the little label attached to the bottle of herbal Viagra. "You little."

I scream when he lunges for me.

"I'll show you who needs dick cream, you little twat."

I laugh as he pins me on the bed, tickling me along my sides and thighs with his fingers. "I just thought, because you're an old man no... AAAAH!" He bites my hip and we wrestle for power. Me still laughing my arse off as he flips me over, rips my trousers down and penetrates me in one powerful swoop.

My laughter stops soon after and, in its place, comes moaning and cursing. I squeeze my eyes shut and push back against him.

When we orgasm, we orgasm together but then I panic and pull away. I race into the shower, remove my clothes and spray my vagina without shame.

"I'm going to need another morning-after pill." I sigh gravely when Sargent stands in the doorway laughing at me. "We've got to stop being so careless."

His laughter stops and dims to a gentle smile. "Aren't you at the doctor's tomorrow for birth control?"

I nod. "I'd almost forgotten. I put it in my phone."

"I'll take you."

"No, it's fine." I smile kindly. "I already asked Fidget. It's during my lunch break."

"Whatever makes you happy," he says, stepping under the water and holding me from behind. He massages my sensitive breasts, paying extra attention to the piercing, as his lips move along my shoulder. "We should look into getting you a car and license."

"I have a British license but I'm only here for another four months."

He tenses and kisses my shoulder. "Perhaps we can do something to elongate that? If you wanted to stay of course."

"Are you asking me to stay?" Hope swells in my chest. Could he be? Does he love me that much? Will I stay if I can?

"I don't know, I don't want you to feel pressured. Let's just take it one step at a time."

I nod and sag against his chest.

"So." He clears his throat. "Will you be smoking some *wacky backy* later, as you call it?"

I know what he's asking for, this is why I giggle and turn in his wet arms. My fingers trace the tattoo that spans from the back of his right shoulder, to his hip and across some of his spine. It's incredible. He's incredible. "I'll do anything you want, it's your birthday, just say the word."

"You are too good to me."

"I love you," I admit, telling him for the second time and it's true. I do. With all of my heart. Maybe it's naïve but who cares? This feeling is amazing, why wouldn't I cherish every moment while it lasts? "I'd do anything for you."

Something flickers in his eyes, something akin to remorse. "Tempest, I..."

"Happy birthday to you!" Devon's loud voice calls from out of the room.

I bite my lip and groan. "I really wanted to have more sex."

"Later." Sargent kisses me and gives me a gentle shove out of the shower.

I quickly dry, dress, and race to meet Devon downstairs before he comes looking for us.

"Morning, Pest," he says kindly but then his smile falls. "What's wrong? You look troubled."

I am troubled. I can't get the look on Sargent's face out of my head when I told him I loved him and he didn't say it back. Maybe he was trying to? No... it wasn't that kind of look. It was one of regret.

Why do I get the horrible feeling this is all going to blow up?

My earlier thoughts on love suddenly feel extremely naïve. I don't want to feel this way, not if it isn't reciprocated. I'm such a child.

No, I'm likely being silly as he just asked me to stay not long ago. I'm reading into shit which is not something I typically do. I've always been a go-with-the-flow kind of girl.

I'm tarnishing the beautiful moment where he told me he loved me, by no longer trusting him and by questioning him. So I settle down and decide to throw him the best birthday imaginable.

By the end of the night, when he's thoroughly spent, and we've had an amazing day together, I figure I made the right call.

15

Tempest

"**B**abe, wake up," Sargent demanded as he ripped the blanket off my body.

"What's wrong?" I blinked sleepily, peering around the dark room. "What time is it?"

"It's past one in the morning, you need to get dressed."

My panic skyrocketed. "Is it Maddox? Is he okay?"

"He's fine... it's us," Sargent said quietly. "The FBI are on their way."

"What?" I squeaked, diving out of bed, wondering if this was all a horrible nightmare.

It wasn't a nightmare.

The FBI showed up minutes later and arrested Sargent. I screamed as they held me back and slammed him to the ground roughly. They handcuffed him but he didn't speak, just looked at me with sad eyes.

They turned over his house, even going so far as to empty the pool and I was just made to sit there as they did so. They asked me questions but I didn't answer. I didn't speak. I didn't say a word.

Because of that they arrested me too and Sargent... well he reacted in a way that got him Tasered.

"SHE'S GOT NOTHING TO DO WITH THIS!" he bellowed, fighting against them. "Tempest, I am so sorry. Look at me. I'm sorry. I'm going to get you out of this, okay? I promise."

I begged them to stop when they pinned him again, telling him it was his fault, he was making it harder on himself.

Seeing him there, stuck as they degraded him in such a way. It was so unnecessary.

They asked me questions, if I took drugs, was he my pimp, shit that made no sense. Then, two hours later, they released me. Just like that. Even though the entire time I didn't say a word. Not even when one of them called me a *smart girl*.

Smart for not speaking? Who knows.

Sargent

Maddox called the cops when he discovered the extra containers were carrying drugs. I thought I raised him to be smarter than that. Perhaps he thought I didn't know.

Why didn't he come to me?

I wait impatiently for them to release her. Those fucks really thought they could use her to get me to confess my crimes? I haven't committed any crimes beyond being duped myself at age nineteen. Since then it has been about survival.

Those pricks tried everything in the book. "Your girlfriend is in there right now spilling all of your secrets. She's told us everything about you and your little scheme."

She doesn't know shit but kudos to them for trying to trap me into saying something incriminating. It might've worked on a guiltier person.

My rage returns tenfold when my lawyer exits through a door with a shaken-up Tempest under his arm.

I move to her and scoop her into my arms. She doesn't protest, only buries her face in my neck and breathes quietly. I exit the building, glaring at Agent Samuels as I pass, who nods knowingly at me. This is all fucked up. None of this was supposed to happen yet.

FUCK.

Maddox...

What have you done?

"I've got you," I whisper in her hair and follow my long-time lawyer, Feinstein, to his car.

"She doesn't even have shoes on. That goes against so many human rights laws. I will personally be putting in a complaint about that," he grumbles, and I have to agree.

I am livid. Absolutely livid.

I lower her into the back seat and climb in after her.

She doesn't speak, I wonder if she's in shock. She screamed for me when those fuckers pinned me and Tasered me. I damn near pissed my pants. Thugs. It was severely unnecessary.

"You did good, kid," Feinstein tells Tempest. "Samuels said she didn't speak a word. Not a single word. Not even her name."

I relax. "Good, then they can't implicate her."

"They didn't read me my rights," she says so quietly I hardly hear her.

"Would you swear on that?" Feinstein asks hopefully.

"I just want to go home," she murmurs, looking out of the window. "I've never been arrested before. Is this going on my record?"

"No," I promise her. "You didn't do anything wrong."

"And you did?" She looks so tired and sad. "What's going on, Sargent? What happened?"

"Nothing we can talk about here," I reply softly, kissing her forehead. "I'm so sorry."

I call my people, my staff, my son, repeatedly. This is going to be such a shit storm.

My house is trashed, well and truly. My lawyer takes pictures of the damage as I return to Tempest in the car. She shifts away from me and sniffles softly, I see the reflection of a tear trail on her cheek.

"We'll go to a hotel." I try to place my hand on hers but she slides it away and uses it to wipe her eyes.

"Where's Maddox?" Her voice is scratchy, probably from the screaming earlier. She was terrified for me.

"We'll find him."

When Feinstein returns, the roar of a bike ascends my steep driveway. I turn and look out of the back window of the car and he appears on his Harley.

Stone pulls up far too close and rips off his helmet.

I climb out of the car, leaving Tempest where she is and instruct her to lock the doors.

"Got the feds turning over my compound. Wanna tell me what the fuck is going on?" He looks angry, and high. Not a good combination.

"Somebody in my company unfortunately discovered a crate and called the police," I explain calmly.

"Who?"

"It doesn't matter."

His eyes narrow, he's never intimidated me, not until this moment when I find myself without a weapon, in just shorts, sneakers, and a white T. He's as big as I am and far more psychotic. I'm not liking my odds. "I asked, *who*."

"They have been dealt with," I reply and find myself pinned against the side of the car with his hands fisting in my T, gripping the fabric and pulling it up to my neck as he tries to cut off my air supply with his knuckles.

"I ASKED WHO!"

I hear the car door open and close.

"Stop!" Tempest yells and Stone's grip on me loosens just enough for me to shove him away. He goes back a step but his eyes stay on me. "Please. I can't take anymore tonight. He'll still be here tomorrow for you to kick the shit out of. I just need a joint and I need a bed."

That took an interesting turn.

"Definite old lady material," Stone mutters and his anger slowly dissipates as he takes in Tempest's appearance. "Where the fuck are her shoes?"

"They arrested her without them and turned over the house."

"Why they take her?" His anger is back but for a different reason this time.

"Because they're dicks. Why else?"

"Fuck." Stone pushes his hair back and shakes his head. "This shit is getting too hot."

"Whatever this is, if you think they're not listening in right now you're both idiots," Tempest snaps. "And for the record, I have fuck all to do with it. Whatever *it* is."

We both look at her and then at each other. I wince because she's right and he looks around, his nose high as he tries to peer through the dark shrubbery that surrounds my property.

"Mr. Wolf." Feinstein leaves the house and strides to us, his face a grim mask. "All of that priceless art work, they've trashed it. I will nail them."

"Dirty fucking cops," Stone grumbles and returns to his bike. "I want a name, Wolf. So will the Russian whore. If she wasn't coming before, she is now."

He clips on his helmet, winks at Tempest, and then the bike roars to life.

"Call me when you're ready to talk."

We wait for him to disappear before climbing into the car. I call my people, all of them, and demand they find Maddox. If I don't get to him before Stone and Nastya do, we are fucked. They will kill him for this.

I've never been so terrified before.

It distracts me from what the fuck I'm going to tell Cassius. He'll never forgive me either.

"Whatever it is," Tempest says softly during the ride to the hotel. She places her hand on my thigh and rests her head on my shoulder. "It'll work out. You'll fix it."

My arm goes around her shoulders and I hold her and accept the comfort she's offering. It helps but only a little, but a little is better than nothing.

～

Tempest

I can't sleep, neither can Sargent. He keeps calling Maddox, and every time there's no answer, I see his panic rise. Even I don't know where he could be at this point.

I hope he's safe.

"Are you sure he hasn't been arrested?" I ask, chewing on the nail bed of my thumb.

"Yes, Feinstein assured me he hasn't been taken in."

"I want to know, but then I also don't," I say softly. "How bad is it?"

The look he gives me makes me cringe. I want to demand answers as to why this is happening but I can't. It would only implicate me. Whatever he's into is his thing and I want no part of it.

But I can't just be blind to everything. I need to know what it is he's a part of.

"You're not trafficking women, are you?" I blurt and his lips part.

"That's the first worst thing you think of when you look

at me?"

"You don't think of women much beyond their vaginas."

He doesn't reply for a long time and I fear the worst. "It's not women, I'd never..." Now I feel awful for asking.

"You can tell me, if you want to. I'm listening."

His eyes shine with an unfathomable look. I wonder if it's vulnerability laced with regret but it's fleeting and I'm too burdened by my own emotions to try and pick his apart. "No judgment?"

"No judgment."

He blows out a long and heavy sigh.

"My ex-wife has always been adventurous with heavy drugs. She dabbled and sometimes so did I. We were stupid and thought it would be okay." His throat bobs as he gulps, trying to find the courage to go on. "I stopped when Maddox was conceived, she couldn't. I didn't realize how far she'd fallen. I got cocky and busy starting up the company with Cassius. We were making money but not enough to get to where we needed to be. My ex-wife's ties with a local drug dealer helped get the money to front my company, so long as I paid them twenty percent of my personal earnings."

"Shit," I mutter, not liking where this is heading.

"Nobody knows, not even Cassius."

And he's telling me? Does that mean he trusts me or does he really need it off his chest?

"When business took off a few years later, Yaroslava, literally the fucking leader of the Russian mafia, decided to take Maddox."

Every single part of me tenses. My heart thuds against my ribs.

"Does Maddox know?"

"He was four, I doubt he remembers, I've never asked as he was unharmed and was covered in ice cream and cake crumbs when he was returned. Yaroslava was simply showing me how easy it would be for him to take my family from me before he made a proposition that changed everything." His hands fist and his jaw clenches. "I'd already paid him back what I borrowed and more through our twenty percent, but now..."

"Is this something to do with the extra container Maddox was talking about a while ago?" It's not hard to put two and two together at this point.

"You knew he was scoping something out?"

I startle at his anger and stare at him, gaping, before snapping, "He just thought it was a mistake and then he never really mentioned it again. I told him to speak to you but I think he wanted to impress you. What was in the crate?"

"Drugs," he replies simply. "Weapons. You name it."

"Jesus," I murmur. "Well if Maddox thinks you're behind it he'll never come back to you. Beyond marijuana he despises drugs."

Sargent's eyes dim with defeat and he slides down the wall until his rear hits the floor. "I need to find him before they do."

"That's the deal you were trying to gamble out of? Is Stone the leader?"

He shakes his head. "He's as good as. He runs the operation with his club. If he backs out, Yaroslava will have a hard time finding people to keep it going."

"What does this mean for it all now?"

"Now that the feds are involved? It'll never go again. My freights will be constantly searched."

Is there a glimmer of hope in there somewhere? "That's good right?"

"No, because Cassius will likely force me out, as he should, Maddox could die if I don't figure out a way to keep his name out of it."

"What about you? What will they do to you?"

My eyes fill with tears as I process the information.

"I'm going to book you a flight, I want you away from here as soon as possible," he says after moving to crouch before me. His hands pull mine away from my face and I wonder if he can see the heartbreak he put there. "I don't want to send you away. But it isn't safe. They will use you to hurt me. These people are sick. There's no end game now. Only vengeance. I've just lost him millions in trade."

"I don't want to leave you." I sniff. "And Maddox..."

"I'll take care of my son, but I need you to be strong and do as I ask. If this ever blows over, I'll come for you."

I stare at the graying sky through the window as the sun rises. This is the first time since I arrived in Malibu that it looks gloomy. Or perhaps it's my new mood reflecting on my vision.

"I don't have shoes, or my things, my passport is still at your house." I chew on my lip and wipe at my wet cheeks. "Let me get my belongings and say goodbye to Devon and Fidget..."

"I can't take that chance. I'll call somebody to collect them. Marcy is booking your flight right now."

I wrap my arms around his neck and bury my face there. "I'm so scared, Sargent. I don't want anyone to get hurt."

"Me too," he replies quietly. "That's why I need you gone so I can focus."

"There's something else." I pull away and search his eyes. I don't want to add to his stresses. "I..."

"What is it?"

"I'm late."

His eyes remain the same but his fingers dig into my thighs a fraction harder.

"This isn't the first time though so it's probably not *that* but I just... I needed you to know." In case he's right and he dies. That sounds morbid and horrible but I've never felt fear like this. Everything was perfect and now it's not. "But if I am, what do I do?"

He stares at me for a longer moment, unblinking. His lips part and close and then he stands and rips his hands through his short hair before looking down at me.

"Are you angry?" I ask quietly. "Maybe I shouldn't have said anything."

"I'm not angry." His reply sounds soft and genuine, so I relax. "Just because you're carrying it doesn't shift the blame to you. I should have known better. It was inevitable."

He's not angry or upset like I expected him to be.

"If you are, we'll figure it out, but right now, I can't think about that. I need you out of here, okay? Yaroslava's psychopathic daughter is in America and she could be here already. She's bitchy and bitter and you're a million times prettier and younger than her so you *need* to go."

I stand and he envelops me in a warm hug.

"If you are, whatever you choose, it's your body and your decision and I will support you," he whispers. "But, you mustn't contact me until I contact you. Do you understand?"

At his words, I shudder with emotion and hold him tighter. "I don't want to leave."

"You must."

"I know, but I don't want to." We rock together in the steadily rising sunlight before he pulls away and makes more calls, calls to get me the shit I need.

16

Tempest

Four hours later, I'm on my way to the airport with one of his security guys and I can't stop replaying the past twenty-four hours in my head.

He didn't freak out at the possibility of my pregnancy. He didn't get mad or tell me to abort. He told me he'd support me. He says I'm his weakness.

I love him. Despite the shit he's in. And Maddox... I'm so worried for him I wish he'd answer his phone.

It's my number now, surely he should recognize it? He knows I have nothing to do with this. What if they already have him?

I push that thought away and chew on my nail bed again. A bad habit I've picked up lately and intend to stop doing as soon as I'm out of the country.

It hasn't sunk in yet. I really don't want to leave but what choice do I have? He's right. I'll just complicate the situation.

So why has he just texted me?

Sargent: You can come back home. It's done. They have their guy.

I try to call him as I frown at his message on the screen. I look to the man on my right.

"Something doesn't feel right about this." If it's not him texting me then does that mean they have him?

"What's wrong?" my driver slash security personnel asks calmly.

"I just got a text message from Sargent asking me to go back."

He takes my phone from my hand and carefully looks at the message. His eyes flicker to the road and back to the phone. "I have to take you to the airport."

"I know," I reply. "I don't think it's him."

His brows furrow with his own anxieties and suspicions as he connects to the Bluetooth in the car and calls the contact, "Bossman."

Unfortunately, Bossman doesn't answer and neither do two other guys who he calls immediately after.

"Fuck," he mutters. He presses something in his ear and speaks a bunch of military-sounding jargon that I don't understand. Then he starts yelling, which turns to begging. He looks at me and I know he's thinking the worst too. "I'm taking you to the airport and seeing you on that plane. Don't argue with me, I'm not in the mood."

I nod once because I don't want to add to his plate either. But then, after building up the courage to challenge a stranger I ask, "But what if they need help?"

"*You* are my priority."

"You're not getting paid if he's dead," I retort firmly, hoping the money will entice him to do what I want him to.

He frowns. "I don't give a fuck. If I take you back there and you end up dead that'll be on my conscience. Not everything is about money. I care about the people I protect."

For the first time in hours I smile, it's weak but it's there. "You're a good person, Miles."

"I need to concentrate," he grumbles and flips his sunglasses over his eyes.

I take that massive hint and turn away, pleading with God, if he exists, to figure this out. I know I'm in way over my head and I should be gratefully running for the hills but I never was very good at staying away from danger. Maddox doesn't deserve this. What if he needs me? He'd never leave me behind.

But I don't know where he is so how can I help?

I want to cry.

I don't know how to handle all of this.

Sargent

I kick a shirt to the other side of my closet and sigh gravely. Especially when I see her underwear beneath it next to an open tube of deodorant. Weeks ago I'd have been furious at the sight, annoyed by the clutter, but it hasn't been something that has bothered me in the slightest.

I think of the products I purchased for her myself for my

personal en suite so when we showered together she'd smell of lavender or berries. I think of the way she dropped her clothes onto my floor and all I'd do is step over them. She'd pick them up eventually, once changed or showered, but it never bothered me.

And now, her things linger and she's gone and I remember why I hated the clutter.

My house is a mess because of the feds and her things are everywhere, reminding me of her every moment. It makes me feel nauseous and bitter. I want her back. I want all of this to go away so I can pin her to the couch and insist she nap with me, before taking her to the store and buying her everything she looks at so she can fill my home with more clutter to remind me of her.

You know you're growing fond of a woman when you want them to nap with you, not fuck you. Though I wouldn't mind that either.

"Any news?" I ask my head of security, Tucker. He's at the door, his shoulders against the frame.

I brush past him and he follows, his hand on his gun. "None yet. Which is good because it means they don't have him."

Hopefully Samuels will have stricken his name from the database. He's the only fed I trust and rely on. He said he would do all he could but he couldn't promise anything. It all depends on those who handled the case, if they were dirty or not. Chances are at least one of them would have been and the name would have been passed back to Stone's boys.

Maddox... what the hell have you done?

When I hear the roar of a bike in my driveway, Tucker steps

in front of me and radios to his companions who are circling my property. "We have company. Be ready."

I peer at the window at the fifteen bikes turning in my front yard so as to be facing the right direction when they need to escape. Stone is leading them but only he and two others enter my house without permission.

"We were wondering when you'd be back," Stone yells and it echoes around my home, bouncing off the windows and white walls.

I descend the stairs and greet him at the bottom.

"We're to keep you here until Nastya arrives." He glances at the cleaning crew who are working through the living area and whistles loudly. "Fuck off upstairs."

The two women and one man all nod and take their things up to my room. At least I'll have something clean to crawl into later if I'm not dead.

"This isn't necessary," I growl, annoyed that I'm being forced into staying. "If you simply called when she arrived, I'd have come. I have nothing to hide."

"Well then this should go easily enough." Stone grins and walks to the refrigerator.

"The feds emptied it," I say when he peers inside looking for beer.

"Those fuckers." He nods to the guy on his left. "Go down the hill and get a crate and something strong. We're gonna need it." We share a knowing look. "Especially if the psycho bitch is coming. Didn't you tap that?"

I nod, fighting back my grimace.

"Yeah?" He shakes his head. "Me too. Fucking crazy and I know crazy... or at least I thought I did."

Nastya wasn't bad, she was just different. Rough, aggressive, liked to be in control and use her teeth a lot. Liked being spanked and called me Daddy. It was a bit weird. Still satisfied me enough to go back a couple of times. Never again.

"She call you Daddy?" he asks and roars with laughter when I nod. "Yeah, I had to toss her out of my bed. Couldn't be doing with that shit."

I don't reply to that because my mind is now elsewhere. "Why have you brought your entire club to my house, Stone?"

"I don't trust the feds not to turn up again. They've scattered to watch the area. My club has been tossed too. They know we're working together so it's just a matter of time before we all go in."

That makes sense. "Please don't leave blood stains on my walls."

"Can't make promises when I don't know your position in this." He smiles dangerously. "Seems a bit suspect to me that you're trying to get out of your deal weeks before the feds are called."

"I had nothing to fucking do with this."

"That's why you won't give us a name?"

Shit. "I'm not giving you a name because it's not the idiot's fault. They were doing what any normal person would have done when finding a crate full of drugs and weapons."

He nods thoughtfully. "But you know we can't let it slide. If word gets out that all they gotta do is call the pigs to get out of a deal, we'll be out of business by the mornin'."

A good point.

We sit in silence for a while, I take my phone out of my pocket and look for messages from Tempest. I told her not to get in touch, but I hate the fact she hasn't. It's better this way.

We don't speak again to each other until his buddies returns with alcohol which I accept easily. I need something to take the edge off.

"Where's that pretty little thing you've been keeping to yourself? Tempest was it?" Stone asks suddenly as I sip my whiskey and clear my throat to help ease the burn.

"We aren't together," I lie. "She was a fling that ended."

His eyes narrow but he doesn't reply as the sound of a car pulling into the driveway has my body becoming solid cement.

Nastya is here.

Tucker moves to me, uneasy at the situation. He's not out of his depth but he is outnumbered.

"You know the rules," Stone says, and Tucker, his men, myself, and Stone's men all place our phones on the TV stand.

We're patted down for wires and other devices as Nastya's heels click on my wooden floor.

"Sargent," she announces, her tone saccharine and fake.

She approaches me on three-inch pumps, her legs narrow and long. She's only an inch shorter than me with the heels. Her dark red hair is pulled back so tight into a high ponytail that the skin around her small eyes seems stretched.

"Sargent," she repeats, hugging me.

I place one arm around her bony waist and ignore the way the shoulder pad of her gray jacket digs into my neck.

"It's nice to see you again, even considering the circumstances," she declares with a heavy Russian accent, then leans forward to kiss my lips. "How have you been?" When she moves away to look around my damaged house she tsks. "The police think they do what they like. Bastard pigs. Such beautiful things now trash."

"How can I help you, Nastya?"

"Business is not great now." She sits on my sofa and the woman who trailed in after her hands her a bottle of water which she sips before handing it back. Her dull brown eyes come to mine. "What will we do I wonder?"

"I don't know but the freights are off-limits for obvious reasons." I try to sound apologetic but it comes off far too firm. I'm not helping myself here.

"Yes, I find it odd though, that this all comes so soon after you try to get out of our deal." She stands again and steps into my space, so she can trail her nail along my jaw. "And you declare innocence yet the first thing you do is send the petite girl to her own country."

My body tenses but I force a laugh. "She was arrested beside me, she fled the moment she got the chance."

When she taps on her phone and holds up a picture of me kissing Tempest goodbye outside of my hotel, I raise a brow and shrug.

"Your excuse?" Nastya asks, her tone teasing and malicious.

"Should I have kicked her out of the door? She was a good fuck."

"I bet she was," Stone mutters and her eyes and mine shoot to him. "Her body was fucking gorgeous. Just wanted between her thighs."

"Have her," I say through gritted teeth. The words make me feel sick. "I've been done with her for a while. Too needy."

Nastya touches my throat, the sharp point of her nails strokes the skin across my jugular. I've heard she's killed men with a similar strike so I quickly grab her wrist.

"Don't tease me," I say quietly, daringly. Wanting her to think I still find her desirable.

It works, I see her eyes flash with interest and lust. "Dare I?"

She wraps her arm around my neck and pushes her tongue into my mouth, just like old times. I reciprocate because at this point I don't have much of a choice. It's tasteless and does nothing to excite me.

"We have an audience," I say, pulling back and resisting the urge to wipe my lips.

"Shame." She sits back on the couch and smiles, her dark lipstick smudged around her lips and mine. "Did I mention Daddy will be here soon?"

Stone and I both tense at that. She better be kidding.

He's a wanted criminal. Surely he wouldn't be so stupid? Or perhaps he will be?

"So this house needs to be put back together and checked for wires." She blinks at Stone and his face falls but he nods like the dutiful little lapdog and his men come in to help the cleaning crew.

Nastya sits and plays on her phone as I drink more whiskey at the counter in the kitchen.

When she appears beside me, I jolt and she cackles unattractively. "You look nervous, Sargent. I wonder why."

"A lot is going on, Nastya, we aren't all emotionless bitches like you," Stone snaps, coming to my aid though only for a moment because she pulls a gun on him. It's a small Glock but it's aimed at his head.

Suddenly everybody in the room has their guns out. Everybody but me.

"Speak to me like that again, you greasy limp dick, and I'll put you down right here," she snarls and I just know she's not kidding.

Stone grins and steps closer, the gun is now only inches from his skull. She'll do it too and I'll end up shot in the crossfire as this room lights up like the Fourth of July.

I place my hand on her wrist and push as my nose skims her hairline. "You're truly going to risk your life to kill this dumb fuck?"

She sighs and then smiles before turning in my arms and pushing the gun back into her jacket pocket. It isn't even secured in a sheath of some kind, it's just hanging in her pocket. Fucking crazy bitch.

"Come, let's move to a quieter room," she whispers and I wish I'd just let them all kill each other.

Stone pats my shoulder as I'm led upstairs, past the sofas on the balcony and straight into my room which is spotless thanks to the cleaners. They did what they could on such short notice.

As soon as the door closes behind me she's attacking my mouth, her nails are scraping against my chest and my back is against the unforgiving wood. I return her kiss but only for a moment. It's not getting me off at all and it feels wrong. I feel as though I'm betraying Tempest.

"I'm surprisingly not in the mood," I explain, stepping around her.

She looks insulted, her massive ego can't handle the rejection.

"Because of that little girl you have been fucking?" She is not happy but I stay calm.

"No, because I haven't slept all night and I'm worried about my future and the future of my company."

Her eyes narrow further. "I traveled all this way to see you and help you with my father and you turn me away like this?"

Fuck. "Like I said..."

"Like the last time when I offered to stay for longer and you declined me then too. Yet now you live with a girl half your age." She pulls out her phone and grins maniacally. "She isn't even pretty."

My lips thin to a white line. "Beauty is in the eye of the beholder, Nastya."

"She's not prettier than me."

Insecure bitch. When I don't reply her cheeks pink with rage.

"I will have them bring her to me right now. I will not be embarrassed by you for anyone! Especially not little girls."

My heart rate picks up. She would be so callous and cruel. What do I do?

"You are still the most beautiful woman I've ever seen, Nastya. I simply don't wish to date you because of your father being who he is. I saw what he did to the last man you tired of."

She laughs at that and cups my face with her hands. "Then we mustn't tell him, yes?"

My stomach is twisting in knots, I feel ill. I feel trapped. I have to be careful not to anger her. If I can stall her for long enough.

"Come," she says, draping her jacket over the chair by my desk. "Now we can fuck."

"I'm not..."

"Release some of that tension." She circles me like a vulture and starts rubbing my back. I close my eyes but there's no willing this away. "We had fun, let us repeat."

Her nails scratch the surface of my arm as she comes to stand in front of me. I let her lift my shirt over my head, begging for an excuse that doesn't sound pathetic and useless. I could say I have an STI but then she'd lose interest entirely and I need her on my side when her father shows up. If he shows up. She's the only one that can keep me alive.

Her fingertips touch the part where my tattoo meets my shoulder, trail across my throat and then dance to my nipple which tightens immediately.

"Come," she whispers against my lips, tugging on my belt to have me follow before undoing it. She scrapes her nails over the top of my jeans but it doesn't even stir.

Fuck. She's going to be really pissed off if I can't get it hard.

I'm going to have to do this. The thought makes me ill but I'm going to have to do it. It's the only way.

I crush my lips to hers, praying for some kind of divine intervention.

Unfortunately, none comes and after discretely rubbing my cock with my birthday gift from Tempest, I make Nastya remember everything she liked about me.

17

Tempest

Tears blur my vision as I'm dragged past the rows of bikes by a humongous, bald-headed dickhead. He's taller than Sargent and has his hand fisted in my hair.

"Gently, Sergei," my captor snaps at his bald-headed guard.

My captor being a very Russian, much older man called Yaroslava. The same man that Sargent told me about just last night.

I don't beg anymore, not like I did for the first five minutes, insisting I had nothing to do with this. Yaroslava pushed a blade against my neck and that's all it took to silence me for the journey here. I would have been safer hiding somewhere. They stopped us en route to the airport. They left Miles by his car in a bloody pulp after this bald fuck and another guard kicked the shit out of him. He put up a good fight but it wasn't enough. I don't even know if he's alive.

"We do not want her as bald as you by the time we make it inside." Yaroslava laughs loudly at his own joke.

Pain grips my scalp as his hand leaves my hair and all of my roots fight to return to their original resting spaces.

I whimper when his strong grip moves to my arm and yanks me into the house where men are scattered in all uniforms. Some in cuts, some in suits, some in casual attire.

They all look our way and they part as I'm shoved through. Their chatter now silent, so silent I can hear something else. Something that sickens me. The sound of a woman's moans of pleasure coming from upstairs. How can anybody be having sex at a time like this?

She's so loud.

"Sit," Yaroslava commands me and I'm pushed toward the sofa facing the stairs.

I sit and the big guy stands behind me as Yaroslava greets Stone and the others in here.

"Clear out," his other guard demands.

"Except you," Yaroslava says to Stone who is eyeing me warily.

Stone nods politely and his men filter out.

"Who the fuck is this asshole?" Yaroslava laughs, pointing at Sargent's head of security.

Stone tells him as much and Yaroslava sighs and raises his silenced weapon. I hear a small noise and watch Tucker drop to the ground lifeless. A bullet between his eyes.

I scream, a reaction I can't suppress but the man behind me clamps a hand around my mouth.

"Shut up," he barks at me as my tears fall onto the side of his hand. He pinches my nose until I start clawing at his wrist. My chest tightens with pain.

"Was that necessary?" Stone asks Yaroslava who just grins, his wrinkled face stretching to his eyes.

The hand leaves my mouth and I choke for air as, finally, a door upstairs opens and a disheveled-looking Sargent and a red-haired woman both descend the stairs less than a minute later.

I pray another man joins them and Sargent just went up to get them but I can see the lipstick around his mouth. I can see the evidence of his erection through his jeans, I can see a dark hickey on his neck. My heart, already shattered, evaporates and all emotions leave me. I think I'm in shock.

"Daddy!" the woman cries, racing to Yaroslava and throwing her arms around him.

They speak in Russian and I'm surprised by how fond of his daughter he is. I keep looking at them because I can't handle looking at Sargent. The images of him and her are in my head. The images of a man dying moments before are too.

So much is happening, I can't process any of it.

"Wait." The woman looks at me. "This is her?"

I stiffen when she stalks my way in heels so high I wonder how she's not broken an ankle yet.

"I just fucked your boyfriend," she states, grinning and watching for my reaction with soulless brown eyes.

"He's not my boyfriend, I hardly know him," I reply, my throat scratchy and sore.

She frowns at my defiance as I hold her gaze. "Shame, I always did like a cat fight."

I stay quiet and glance over at the lifeless legs just visible from the side of the couch. My body tries to heave but I force it back.

"Leave Tempest alone, Nastya," Yaroslava demands. "Somebody bring the girl a whiskey, she's trembling."

"No, thank you," I reply, thinking that if I am pregnant, I don't want to hurt it anymore than the stress of this situation already is.

"Drink," Yaroslava snaps and Nastya returns to me with the bottle. She pushes it hard against my lips, holding my head in place by my hair. When it filters into my mouth I start choking again and push her hand away so hard the bottle drops to the ground and smashes.

I feel her palm against my cheek, a sting, followed by the ringing of my ear. She just slapped me.

I glare at her as a handprint bubbles on the surface of my skin. I don't touch it, I don't give her the satisfaction.

"Nastya," Yaroslava says but sounds more amused than annoyed as he pulls his daughter to his side and then pushes her behind him. "Now, to business."

I look at Sargent who is being restrained by Stone and the other guard that escorted me here. He's red-faced, I've never seen him so angry. Is that because of what she did? Why does he care? He was just fucking her.

"I'm going to ask you personally as you haven't been forthright with Mr. Stone," Yaroslava states, pulling his gun back out and twisting it in his hands. "Give me the name of the person who told our tales and if we investigate your innocence, we might let you go. Nearly twenty years of loyal service between us means I'm willing to be reasonable. To a point."

"The person has been dealt with," Sargent replies and I hear the desperation in his tone.

"I doubt that." Yaroslava raises the gun to Sargent's head and laughs loudly. "This is why I brought her. I had thought she meant more to you but finding you in bed with my only daughter has me questioning her usefulness. Still..." I watch as the long cylinder barrel of the gun slowly moves my way until it's pointing directly at my eyes.

"No... she's innocent," Sargent yells. "Truly she has nothing to do with this."

"Neither did he." He nods to the body by the couch and the guard behind me chuckles as though this is a TV show and not real life. We're nothing but cattle to these people. "Tick tock, Mr. Wolf. A name, please."

"He made a mistake," Sargent yells, pulling forwards but he's being held too tightly. "He did what anybody would have done."

"Who?" Yaroslava asks calmly, his mask still one of happiness. He's so fucked up. "Not why, Mr. Wolf, but who?"

I look down the barrel of the gun, wishing this would all just be over.

Sargent doesn't reply, of course he doesn't, it's Maddox. I'd never expect him to choose his son over me and Maddox is my life. I'll never give him up either.

Yaroslava lowers the gun and an evil smirk creeps across his lips and flashes in his brown eyes that are just as soulless as his daughter's. "Perhaps he needs a little more incentive?"

Nastya claps her hands and nods to Stone. "Have him fuck her."

My teary eyes go to Sargent who looks at me, panicked and likely as terrified as I am.

"I don't rape women, not my style," Stone states, raising a hand as his eyes too come to me. "Doesn't get me off."

"No matter," Yaroslava says with a shrug and I feel the bald-headed bastard's hand in my hair again. "Sergei loves to take women."

"No," I yell when he clamps an arm around my waist and brings my back to his body. I struggle, clawing at his arm as he holds me tight. "Let me go."

"The couch will do, Sergei."

Sergei turns me and grins in my face. My body hits the couch with a jarring thud that sends pains shooting through my neck, burning the muscles that protect it.

"Let me go," I beg. "Please... stop!" I kick out as he grips my jeans and rips open the button without so much as a yank. The little metal circle hits the wood floor and rolls away.

"If you don't take your hands off her..." Sargent yells as my jeans are tugged down. I feel the air hit my rear as I try to crawl away.

This is humiliating, terrifying, I don't want to be here anymore. Just end it. It needs to be over.

"That's enough," Stone bellows and I feel his hands under my arms, yanking me off the couch and away from the guy that smells of petrol.

He glares at us both as Stone pulls my shaking form into his side, bending to slide my jeans back up to hide my modesty.

"I won't be a party to this, Yaroslava," he snarls. "This is not how we do shit. Not in my fucking city."

"Such sensitive little creatures in the States," Nastya says while rolling her eyes.

I heave when I see Sergei palming himself over his trousers. My hand grips the back of Stone's shirt. I'm going to faint.

"You already have the name, you already know who has done this so why fucking toy with an innocent woman?" Stone yells.

"Innocent?" Nastya laughs loudly, her tone a screech against my humming eardrums. "She's as innocent as us. Did you know she killed her father and brother when she was only fourteen years old? Murdered them in cold blood. Hardly innocent."

When eyes come to me at that revelation I shrink away. It wasn't my fault. I didn't mean to kill them.

I concentrate on Stone's aftershave and how it smells sweet, but also spicy. It's helping me breathe. I just focus on that and nothing else.

"It was self-defense, Nastya," Sargent replies, glancing at me but I look away before we connect. I don't know how he knows but I suspected he might look into my past. It's not like it's a hidden record. "She paid her dues."

"Whatever." Nastya waves him off and looks around, bored.

Stone shifts secretly and I feel his hand under my ribs, he presses something on his side, something hidden by his clothes. "Yaroslava, you had to know the drug thing is a bust, you made millions out of shipping shit out of the country. It's time to find a new way. We got cocky. Greedy, even, and it was our downfall."

Yaroslava glares at Stone as he spits, "Are you forgetting who you're talking to, boy? I've been running this operation since you were in diapers! My loyalty to your club is the only reason I'm not putting a fucking bullet in your skull right now!"

"It's true, Yaroslava, you might think I'm speaking out of turn but I told you to stop at the drugs, then you brought weapons into it, even missiles. It got too much. Somebody was gonna find out at the rate you were shifting shit, doesn't matter who anymore. It's done. It's over."

"That's all we need," Sargent says, and it sounds completely out of context.

The sound of glass shattering and bullets flying echoes through the next few moments, distorting reality as Stone pins me under his body. I don't scream, I can't even breathe. I want to vomit and faint as men storm the room, the feds.

Bodies drop, bullets fly, people grunt and cry but then it all goes silent.

"Oh shit," I hear Stone murmur and I look up again, just as Yaroslava cries, "NASTYA!" He starts sobbing in Russian as he cradles her to his chest. Blood flows from her throat and even I find the moment emotional.

"WHO?" he bellows, looking around the room.

"You'll see her in a second, you Russian prick." A fed I recognize as Samuels from last night raises his gun and with a bang, Yaroslava is gone, just like that, just like Tucker. "Oops, crossfire casualty."

He high-fives a man beside him who sneers down at the Russian father and daughter before somebody tosses a sheet over their faces.

I turn and dry heave properly this time, needing to vomit but my stomach is empty. Stone rubs my back but I push him away.

"I'm sorry I let it get so far, I needed you to be in a position I could grab and move you," he explains softly.

"That all just happened," I say, looking around the room. The only casualties seem to be on Yaroslava's side. His two henchmen are dead, his daughter, her guards...

I heave again and feel hands on my arms; when I see it's Sargent I shove him away and shout, "Don't you fucking dare. Don't touch me."

"Tempest," he tries. "I can explain."

"I don't want to hear it," I cry. "You're disgusting... how could you?"

"He didn't have a choice," Stone interrupts, defending Sargent like a typical guy.

"There's always a choice," I hiss. He reaches for me again, his hand to my cheek and I almost vomit at the thought of where it's just been. "No. Don't."

"Tempest, please," he whispers but is drawn away by Samuels.

I'm guided away too for my statement and whatever the fuck else. I just want to be gone from here so badly.

Sargent

It's done. The FBI have enough evidence to move in on the Russians. Stone who was wearing a wire has been cleared of all involvement and so have I. But I can't celebrate. Seeing her face, her eyes as I came down those stairs. I broke her. Hell, the entire thing broke me.

I feel as though I can't breathe.

These assholes move around my home, collecting bullets and other evidence.

I'm done with them now; my life is my own again. No more feds, no more drugs, no more mafia, or what's left of it now that the FBI and CIA have enough to get into Russia.

Well, it's mostly over.

I move to where she's standing, her jeans partly open since the button doesn't keep the flaps together, her top crooked and off center with a rip up the side, her hair a mess and her eyes swollen from crying.

My hand lingers in the space between us, she needs to accept my touch. I don't want to upset her any more than she is already. "Temp..."

"Maddox!" she cries and brushes past me and straight into the arms of my son.

Maddox holds her, his chin atop of her head as she turns her face away from me. He doesn't meet my eyes and I know why. He's ashamed of what I've done. If only he knew it was the only way to keep him safe. I did my best. I wasn't greedy, I paid my debts, I was just a naïve kid.

"Maddox," I try, brushing past Samuels who is trying to get my attention.

"Not now, Dad," Maddox replies, his eyes sad as they come to mine. "We'll talk, but not now. Let me get her out of here."

"No," I say firmly and grab his arm. "You're not leaving, not until this is sorted and neither is she. I deserve the chance to explain myself."

"You will," he replies gently as I resist the urge to thread my fingers through her hair and pull her into my arms. Doesn't she see that I need her too? "Dad..."

"I didn't have a choice, Tempest," I try again but she makes no movement to say she has heard me. "You have to believe me."

"Dad, not now," Maddox barks. "Now isn't the time."

Samuels, who has been a party to this one-sided conversation, hands a foil blanket to Maddox and helps him wrap it around her. She doesn't look at me with her vacant eyes or broken expression, she looks at the bodies and then the couch and I beg her mentally to just look at me.

Maddox leads her away with an agent hot on their heels. I wonder if I'll ever see her smile at me again, if she'll ever allow it. The thought burns my throat and eyes. Maddox will understand, perhaps he already does.

"I kept him under witness protection until I figured out who I could trust," Samuels explains looking around the room at his men.

"You could have told me that."

"I couldn't risk anything going wrong."

I can understand that.

"He knows you were trying to get out of it. He'll come around and so will she."

"I fucked another woman less than an hour after she left. She's not coming back."

He shakes his head, his empathy apparent in his features. "If it's worth fixing, then fix it."

"I'm free to leave?" I question, raising a brow as we meet eyes.

"Go. Rest. Get your shit together. We'll talk tomorrow."

She left with Maddox who I soon found out had been put under protection by Samuels himself. That's why we couldn't find him.

It's done, but it isn't. If only they hadn't found her, she'd never have had to know. I didn't want to do it. I didn't come, I didn't enjoy it, I had to.

Or maybe I didn't.

Fuck.

She left in his arms, he carried her out of there as she sobbed against him. He didn't even look at me, just took her and left and I could do nothing but watch.

She deserves better than this, more than what I can give her.

"Donate, destroy, and trash everything," I tell Marcy who places a hand on my shoulder to comfort me.

"Have you called her?" she asks, knowing about the situation as I told her during a drunken rambling last night.

She's the only person speaking to me. Cassius has served me with papers to buy me out of the Malibu business but won't even look at me. Maddox won't even reply to tell me where he or Tempest are and I know they're together.

I don't know anything about anybody and nobody will talk to me.

Nobody but Marcy.

I sit on the sofa as strangers move around my home, carefully packaging salvageable equipment. I need out of this home. It's beautiful but I need a fresh start. Everything reminds me of her. Everything reminds me of the deaths surrounding the choices I made as a teen.

Marcy exits the house when one of the removal people call

for her but she returns less than five minutes later and stands in the doorway. "You should see this, Sargent."

Sighing, I stand and grumble my way to her, wondering what else could be wrong with this fucking house.

The pool is empty, the garden furniture is gone, but the art equipment remains. Or the easel does at least and what stands on it is a nearly finished painting of me, beautifully done with acrylics. Maddox is seven and sitting on my shoulders, leaning over to look at my face.

I clear my throat to shift the lump that's making it hard to breathe.

"What shall we do with this?" Marcy asks softly.

"Nothing, wrap it and store it. That's one thing I'm not parting with." It's the most beautiful painting I have ever seen.

God, I miss her. I miss them both.

Marcy smiles knowingly. "He'll call. He knows it's not your fault. He's just angry."

"I really made a mess of life, didn't I?"

"Yep, but you fixed it too... eventually."

"I fucked another woman and she caught me, I'd hardly call that fixing anything."

Marcy winces. "Just keep trying, she'll reply one day."

"Maybe I should leave her be? She deserves better."

"Hello?" Marcy raises her hands at our surroundings. "That's what you're trying to do isn't it?"

I head back inside, grab my car keys off the counter and go. Not because I have anywhere to be but because I don't and that's extremely frustrating. I need to keep busy.

18

Tempest

It's been a week and I'm still so jumpy, adrenaline still courses through my veins whenever the memory surfaces again. Which is often.

People died. I don't know how to live with that again and this time it wasn't even my fault.

There's just so much going on. I'm busying myself with my art, trying to stay positive and normal for the most part. I'm going back to work for Devon next week. I've got a therapy session thanks to Maddox who won't let me say no though I think his father is behind it.

I just can't talk to him yet. I don't know how.

I'm trying to understand it, to understand him but I can't process it. He had sex with somebody else. Maybe it wasn't for pleasure, maybe it was to keep me safe...

I don't blame him, not entirely, I just don't know how to move past it.

"That's incredibly dark, Pest," Maddox comments, looking over my shoulder at my unfinished drawing.

"I had to get it out of my head."

Tucker's legs peek out from beside the sofa. It's drawn in dark colors, blends of grays and black with some white.

"I get it." Maddox places his hand on my shoulder. "Ice cream?"

"No, thanks."

"You've hardly eaten."

I shrug. "I'm not feeling great."

He sighs and sits on my bed. "Do you want to talk about it?"

Shaking my head, I put my pencil down and look at my gray-stained fingers. "Everything was so perfect and then suddenly... people died in front of me."

"I wish I'd sent you away first before calling the police."

"Me too," I murmur, wetting my lips. "My period's late. Really late. I don't know if it's the stress of everything or..."

He doesn't hesitate like I thought he would. There's no judgment in his eyes either. "I'll get you in with a doctor."

"No, I should speak to your dad. I just don't know how to approach him. Whenever he calls I feel sick and just want to run away."

He pats the bed beside him but I decline, needing space right now.

When there's a knock on the door Maddox stands to open it and Cassius walks inside, a tray in his hands. "I come with coffee and snacks."

"You didn't have to do that, Uncle Cass," Maddox says as the tray is placed on the table by my bed.

"Don't mention it." He looks at my drawing. "That's incredible. So dark... makes me feel uneasy."

"Sorry."

His chuckle is quiet but there. "Why are you apologizing? Art is supposed to make you feel things." Then he clicks his fingers. "Actually, I know the owner of a gallery in the city who would probably love your work. I could put in a word if you like?"

"I've asked so much of you already."

Maddox and he share a look which communicated things I don't understand.

He replies, "you haven't asked me for anything. I'll get bragging rights if you make it big time."

I finally smile, it's weak but it's real and my heart thumps a beat. "Thanks, Cassius. For everything."

Cassius put me and Maddox up that very night. All Maddox did was show up on his doorstep. Cassius stepped to the side and we've been here ever since. He's a great host, a lot nicer than Sargent was in the beginning but I'm finding it hard to bond and make an effort. I don't feel good. Mentally, physically, emotionally.

I'm broken right now.

"Any time," he replies, smiling brightly. He's handsome, but he's not Sargent. "Maddox, can we talk a moment?"

Maddox nods and leaves my room. I continue drawing until my phone rings.

Speak of the devil and he shall appear.

I stare at his name on my phone and chew on the end of my pencil.

Fuck it.

"Hey, Sargent," I say softly as I place my pencil down and breathe slowly.

"Finally," he responds, sounding so relieved I feel guilty for making him wait so long. "I've been worried."

"I know, I'm sorry, I just needed time."

He blows out a heavy breath. "I get that. I had so much to say and now I don't even know where to begin."

"I don't blame you for what happened to me. I want you to know that before you start saying whatever it is."

"What about with Nastya?" he asks cautiously but optimistically. "You have to know I didn't want to do it. If it wasn't for that herbal shit you got me for my birthday I never would have been able to."

I didn't want to know that. "Sarge..."

"No, Tempest, you have to believe that I wouldn't do that. I'm not the kind of man that cheats on my woman."

"Was I your woman?"

I hear him shift, as though changing positions. "What does that mean?"

"It means..." I don't even know what it means. "Why are you trying to get me to understand anything anyway?"

"Why?"

"Yes, why?"

"Because I don't want to lose you."

"Why?"

"Because we're good together."

"That's the only reason?" I just need him to say it. I need to hear the words.

He pauses and then when he speaks, his tone is different,

softer but deeper. "I care for you, very much. You know that. I know you do."

"But you don't love me." Spending this time apart from him has been an eye opener. I've been able to truly look at the past few weeks and see them for what they are. Like the moment he told me he loved me and I'd been so elated I almost missed the regret in his eyes immediately after he said it. Like the next day when I said it back and ignored his flinch and put it off as something else. "Do you? It's one-sided. You're not even sure you ever will."

"Tempest..." He pauses again and I want to demand an answer. "I don't know what to say because I don't want to lose what we have but I also don't want to give you false hope."

"I'm just a time filler, aren't I? I'm just here until you get bored. Which could literally be any day, at any time."

"Isn't that the same for anybody?"

"No, because love doesn't go away overnight on a whim for something newer," I reply. "And after seeing all of that death and all of that drama... I just don't think I want to waste any more time on somebody who can't promise me a future."

"Nobody can promise you that this early on," he insists gruffly.

"You can promise me you won't love me though, can't you?"

Yet again I receive nothing but silence.

"Sargent!" I snap. "Answer me."

"I don't want to lose you."

"I don't want to lose my sanity to you."

He chuckles but I can tell it's forced. "Let me take you to

dinner, we can talk about this face-to-face, clear the air. This should be a conversation in person. Where are you?"

"I'd rather just..." It's hard to say because I don't want to lose him. I don't want to break up with him because I do love him. I shouldn't, I know it. "I'm at Cassius'."

"Cassius'?" His tone darkens again for a different reason this time.

"There's something else, before we fall out because you don't approve of where I'm staying."

"I'm listening."

I take a deep breath in and count to five. "I still haven't gotten my period."

I wait for the explosion, the same one I expected before but it doesn't come.

"Okay, well..." The phone rattles and he clears his throat. "Let's just take a test and see what it says then take it from there."

"In some ways you're so much more mature than me," I mumble and this time he chuckles for real.

"I'll be there in an hour and we'll do a test and go to dinner and take everything how it comes. How's that?"

"That sounds good."

I get showered and change, anxious to get this out of the way and a tiny bit excited to see the outcome. I don't want a baby to come out of this mess. Not now. It's too soon and I feel as though I still have so much life left to live. But then I think about it the other way and wonder what it would be like to be a mother. Perhaps it's a naïve thought but there's a little bit of excitement at the prospect.

What terrifies me the most is how Sargent will react. What if he gets angry or storms away? I'll have to go all the way back to England because I can't afford healthcare here. Will he provide for the baby?

I'm getting ahead of myself but it's nice to have something else to focus on.

When I exit the bedroom I seek out Maddox and Cassius who are speaking in the kitchen.

They stop talking in hushed tones when I step into the room and both of them smile at the sight of me.

"I hope it's okay, Sargent is on his way to pick me up. We're going to talk."

"Good." Maddox smiles and drains the rest of his drink. "It will clear your head."

Cassius nods his agreement. "But tell us if he upsets you and we'll kick his ass." He grins at Maddox. "We can take him if we attack him together."

Maddox doesn't look so sure. "I'll let you do it. I'll bring popcorn."

"So you can be entertained by my ass whoopin'? Not a chance. Sargent would kill me."

I giggle at their banter and pull myself onto a stool. Maddox stands behind me and braids my hair. I'm so lucky to have him in my life.

I tilt my head back so it rests on his chest and accept the hug from behind. Then I wait impatiently for Sargent to arrive.

When he does I hold my breath as Cassius greets him. There are no hard feelings between them. Apparently, they hashed it out but Cassius accepted Sargent's explanations and apologies. Cassius just isn't the kind of guy who holds grudges. Though it would have been different had it all blown up in his face.

He's so handsome, even now while my mind is foggy with depression and shock I can't help but admire how truly gorgeous he is. It's such a shame he feels he can't love. His hair has been cut but his beard is just a couple of millimeters long and so neatly shaped around his cheeks and jaw. There's not a hair out of place.

When he sees me, his eyes soften and he doesn't stop as he strides my way, not for anybody. I'm yanked from my seat and his lips are on mine. For a moment I relax into it and accept it because it's him. But then I remember everything and how I feel and how I know he's going to make me feel so I push him away.

"Let's go," he whispers, his eyes determined as they scan my face.

"Hi, Dad," Maddox says jokingly. "Standing right here."

Sargent turns and hugs his son with one arm as his other hand lingers on mine, as though worried I'll run.

I allow it and allow him to lace his fingers through mine as he leads me from the house. I don't want to cause a scene but the second the door closes behind us I snatch my hand back.

"Don't. I need a clear head," I say as he guides me to his car which is parked in the massive driveway beside Cassius' silver Bentley. "I can't think when your hands are on me."

His answering smile is cocky, arrogant, but so fucking sexy.

I glare because if I don't, I'll climb him like a tree and just say fuck it to everything else that needs resolving.

When I fold my body into the seat, I almost sit on a white

paper bag. He closes my door and rushes to his side as I peek at the contents. Pregnancy tests, three of them.

My heart starts hammering. I figured he'd make me go into a pharmacy myself but he's been a gentleman. I don't know why I doubted him.

"Tests first, or talk?" he asks, reaching over me to grab my seatbelt. His lips brush against mine. That was crafty. It makes me smile.

When we're both buckled in he starts the engine.

"Be pointless talking without any answers."

"I need to know you forgive me for what happened," he says, placing his hand on my thigh. "I don't want you to base your decisions on the fact you think I'm an asshole."

"My decisions?"

"In general. On whether or not you want to continue."

"I get it. I understand why you did what you did. Stone said..."

"You've spoken to Stone?"

I shrug. "He emailed me."

"He emailed you?"

"It's not a big deal. I didn't hear from him again." I place my hand on his that is squeezing my thigh and lift it away before placing it on the console between us. "He just explained what happened with Nastya."

"Don't say her name, it makes my skin crawl." He visibly shudders. "I didn't want to. I needed to get her on my side and she was insistent. When she said Yaroslava was coming and started threatening you. I panicked. She had pictures of you on her phone."

"Did you, *finish?*"

"No... hell I didn't even begin, Tempest. I didn't even remotely enjoy it." He shakes his head as though shaking away the memory. "She's a psychopath that likes to lead men around by their dicks."

"Liked," I murmur because she can't any longer. "I've never been so scared."

"Me neither. When I heard you scream and when you were attacked, I couldn't do anything. They had me and I tried but I didn't want to get you killed."

"That part I understand. You did the best you could, Sargent. You're not a superhero. As much as I'd liked to have seen you lay them all out without getting holes put in you, you're only human and you were outnumbered."

His hand goes back to my thigh but he mutters an apology and removes it. "I've missed you."

"I've missed you too. Or the easy brief life we had together before all of this."

"Amen. How are you doing?"

"Not great. I'm struggling to sleep."

His profile softens with mutual understanding. "Me too."

"Tucker's family..."

"Have been paid. I matched his life insurance and doubled it. He has a daughter, she's thirteen but I've made it so she never has to worry about paying for college."

"Thank you," I murmur, feeling like crying again. I didn't know him but seeing him so coldly murdered for no reason other than amusement has been so hard to get past. I wonder if

I'll ever sleep without seeing his eyes in my mind the second I close my own.

"You look beautiful today." He's being genuine but I know he's using it to change the subject. "I'd really like to keep this going."

"I don't know if I can."

He nods once, his lips a thin line as he maneuvers the car through Malibu and to a small apartment complex near the beach.

"My new home," he says, shrugging. "It's just temporary until something better in the area opens up."

"Good luck with that." I grin and we climb from the car.

He uses a key fob to open the double doors and leads me to the elevator. It clinks and hums as it ascends to the third floor and I try not to look at our reflection in the mirror on the walls.

He keeps an arm around my shoulder and kisses my hair before guiding me out the second the door opens and using a different key to open the door to apartment number eight.

It's small and cozy, with two bedrooms and a balcony that extends from the kitchen to the master bedroom. That makes it easier to get midnight snacks, I guess.

"I'm terrified," I admit, holding one of the boxes in both hands.

"Me too." He takes the box from my hands, opens it, tears open the foil wrapper that hides the stick and then guides me to the bathroom. "You do your business and call me when you're ready."

I close the door, stick in hand and pray I drank enough water on the way to get a steady pee flow.

I pull off the lid, sit on the toilet and bite my lip as I position the correct end of the stick between my thighs. This is going to change everything. I just know it.

I stop mid-pee and quickly put the other one under me too. Then I clip the lid back on and place them side by side on the sink as I wash my hands.

The door opens as I stare at my reflection in the mirror wondering what kind of mother I'll be. Sargent wraps his arms around my waist and kisses my neck. I close my eyes and rock with him as he sways us. I always felt so safe in his arms, not just because of how large he is but he just emits that feeling.

"Why can't you love me, Sarge?"

He sighs grimly and kisses my jaw before looking at my eyes in the mirror. "At my age, love doesn't come too easily. We hold back because we've experienced love in most forms and none of it ended well."

"You're holding back because of the age gap?"

He nods. "I guess I'm worried that in a year you'll wake up and decide you don't want to be with an old man anymore."

"You're not old."

"Not yet, but in a year..." His playful smile is contagious. "We're good, Tempest, the tests are negative."

"What?" I squeak and pick up the stick. My jaw drops, my head spins. "I'm not pregnant?" I don't know how I feel about this. I don't know how I should feel about this.

Tears spring to my eyes, it's an irrational reaction but I'm emotional and confused.

"Did you want to be?" His tone is soft as I drop the stick

into the sink and place my hands on his shoulders. "You look sad."

"I don't know. I don't think so. I don't even particularly want kids. It's just... overwhelming. I'm happy but also sad."

"Me too." His admission surprises me. "I was getting used to the idea."

"You'd be starting all over again if you had kids now." I lock my ankles around the back of his shins. "You've done it all before."

His eyes cast downwards as he imagines the picture I'm painting.

"I still want to travel all over the world..."

"I wouldn't stop you."

I stroke his cheek and kiss his jaw. "I know you wouldn't, but one day I also want to get married and you're not interested in that. You've done that. I might not want kids now but I can't say I won't in ten years. You don't want that either."

"I almost wish you were pregnant now," he says, sighing gravely as his hands tighten on my hips.

"Why?"

"Because you wouldn't be breaking up with me, we'd be having a different conversation right now."

He's right but maybe this is a blessing. We've likely dodged a bullet.

"Can't we just enjoy each other? For a little while longer?" His eyes are so earnest and surprisingly vulnerable in a way I've never seen.

"I'm going to Africa with Cassius."

"Cassius." His tone darkens much like it always does when I mention his closest friend.

"I was waiting to see the outcome of this but yes, I'm going to be on Cassius' personal team."

"I bet you are," he mumbles and I feel immediately irate.

Sargent

The thought of her and Cassius sharing a tent, or a fucking hovel, in a foreign country, fucking and falling in love has me feeling nauseous. Cassius isn't like me, he'll snap a girl like her up and marry her. Especially one who is so much like him in the sense that she wants to save the planet and goes psychotic if you forget to recycle.

I'm losing her and I don't know how to fix it.

"Is something going on with you and Cassius?" I ask stupidly and watch the shutters come down in her eyes. My jealousy overrode my better judgment. "Sorry, I didn't mean that. Word vomit. I just hate the thought of you being with somebody I know when you're done with me."

"We should quit while we're ahead," she tells me and I hate that thought too. "Nothing but hurt is going to come from this, besides, we're so irresponsible together. We've been having unprotected sex like virginal teens for over a month."

"We're passionate, we forget the dull stuff, nothing wrong with that." I look back at our time together fondly. I wonder if she doesn't.

"That *dull* stuff, could change our entire lives."

I shrug. "What do you want then, Tempest?"

"I want to spend the rest of my life with you," she states. "I want you to want the same."

Her answer floors me. "You're young..."

"So? That doesn't mean I don't know what I want, especially with everything that has happened as of late."

She has a point.

"I don't want to get married again," I admit. "And I don't particularly want to be a father again. If it happened, so be it, but it hasn't and I'm not interested in trying."

I want to be honest with her because she needs to know I can't be what she needs. It hurts me to say it but I can't hurt her by lying to her.

"I can't love with the same intensity that you do and because of that I'm never going to be able to give you enough." I wipe away a tear that falls down her cheek. Dipping my head, I kiss her ready lips and press my forehead to hers.

"Well." She exhales a shaky breath. "Thanks for your honesty, I guess."

I kiss her again but she turns her head away.

"I should go."

"Don't," I demand softly, urging her to do things my way, for a little while longer at the very least. "Not yet. Stay with me."

She bites her lip and arousal swims in her eyes as I lower my head and kiss the soft skin of her throat. Her body shivers in my arms so I press deeper, suckling her skin and tasting her with my tongue. Tiny moans leave her parted lips and her body relaxes against me. How badly I want to be inside of her right now.

I grind as my hands grip, and kiss as her head moves, baring her throat to me.

Though when I reach for the hem of her white shirt she grabs my wrist and douses the embers of the fire I'm attempting to stoke.

"Can you give me a ride back to Cassius'?" she whispers, pushing me back gently with both hands.

Fuck. This is it. I've lost her.

I'm not allowed to kiss her anymore, to touch her, to just hold her.

"Say it," I demand, watching her avoid my eyes. "Tell me it's over and I'll take you home."

"What other options are there? I'm leaving soon anyway."

"Say it, Tempest."

"Fine." She looks me dead in the eye. "We're done. No more... shag partners or whatever we were."

The words slice through me but I pretend they don't affect me. "I'll take you home."

"We can be friends? We can email?"

"Maybe." I don't want that. Not at all. I can't even possibly entertain being around her, even digitally.

FUCK.

"Let's go." I lead her out of my apartment, to the elevator and then to my car.

"Oh, your umm... unfinished birthday gift is at the Barbie house."

"Barbie house?"

"Yeah." She smiles, looking at me with eyes twinkling with

amusement. "First time I saw your house I thought Barbie should live there."

I roll my eyes but her amusement is contagious. She's fucking adorable. "Where is it?"

"On the easel in the garden if it hasn't been destroyed. It's nearly done. I can finish it before I go if you can pick it up?"

She's referring to the painting I have in storage until I find the perfect place for it.

"I've seen it. It's divine. I'm unworthy of it."

"Divine? You think so?"

"It's the only thing I kept, I'll cherish it. Maybe one day you can come back and finish it?" We share a smile and I put the car in drive. "So, Africa?"

"I'll be leaving as soon as Cassius allows it."

Which means she's been waiting for my response. Why can't I care about her a little less? Then I could lie to her and tell her I love her and want her to stay. She would. I know she would.

"You could come too?" she suggests, placing her hand on mine, I lace our fingers and rub my thumb over the back of hers.

"Not my thing." Saying that aloud just further proves how perfect for Cassius she is and not me. He's ready for kids, he's ready for a marriage that isn't shit. "Just stay in touch, send me pictures, keep Maddox safe."

"Maddox isn't going. He wants to settle for a while longer."

This makes me feel even worse. "So who's going to look after you?"

"I'll be fine, I was alone for years before Maddox, Sargent. Don't worry."

"I'll always worry about you." I kiss her wrist and fall into silence. "Can we eat before I take you back?"

Tempest

Should I? It feels like torture already. Any longer in his presence and I'll cave. This is best, to end things now while we're amicable and friendly. Not nine months down the line when he's bored and I'm heartbroken. This way won't cause issues with Maddox. I can still be a part of their lives.

"I think it's best this day just end."

"I'm not ready to let you go just yet."

I blink away my heartache at his words and admit, "me neither."

19

Tempest

I haven't seen him for weeks but I've heard his voice when Maddox has spoken to me on the phone. It's hard saying goodbye, wondering if he's moved on already, wondering if I'll bump into him while he's with another woman.

He texted me this morning asking me how I am but I ignored it. I need space and time to get over him.

Thank heavens I'm leaving Friday, with Cassius. We're heading to the Democratic Republic of Congo. It's in no way safe but we're hoping to bring food, water, and land to at least some of the children there. There's already a setup to the east in a village surrounded by barren lands that hopefully, with the help of orange peels and the changing climate, will perk up in the next decade. It's not as though the area isn't full of resources, it's that the locals aren't safe enough to settle down anywhere so they lack the knowhow to get these things safely.

It's something Cassius is truly invested in. His hazelnut eyes light up whenever we talk about it. His vision for the future there is one I want to be a part of. We could be making history as we know it.

We just got confirmation of sponsorship and permission to enter the country. This is exciting but terrifying.

Maddox now wants to come but we talked him out of it. He only wants to come because I'm going but I know his heart lies elsewhere. I think he's met somebody. I'm happy for him, a little bit jealous that his attentions will soon lie elsewhere but happy all the same.

"Yeah, thanks, Marcy, she's basically the same," I hear Cassius say, chuckling as he gets closer to where I'm sitting in the dining room. "Ridiculous, I know."

He hangs up and beams at me from ear to ear when he steps through the open door. "We're going Thursday, not Friday, so get dressed, we need to shop for supplies."

I stand and look longingly at my phone.

I'll call him later.

We head to Devon's and he helps set me up with a backpack perfect for my height and weight.

We have an emotional goodbye, one with tight hugs and promises to keep safe before I head out. I've been working for him again for the past three weeks so we've really bonded.

I'll definitely come back one day to see him.

We visit a military store for long-lasting clothing and shoes and by the time we're both geared up we look ready to join the army. We laugh and joke about it for a while before the reality of where we're going and what we're doing kicks in.

"Nervous?" he asks as we admire our tan combat trousers in the mirror.

I shrug. "Not really. You?"

"Terrified," he admits, grinning.

"You have a lot more to lose than me. I just have myself and my clothes and the ability to move."

He nods thoughtfully. "That's one way to look at it." His arm snakes around my shoulder and squeezes. "We'll be fine. It's not war-torn where we're going. Not terribly anyway."

"I'm looking forward to it. Minus the bugs. So many bugs."

He cringes so I know he feels the same. "Call Sargent, maybe you'll get to see each other before we leave?"

"I will, later. Not now. I don't have my phone."

"That's okay," he pulls his from his pocket and calls his friend. "I have mine. Talk... get changed. I'll meet you out front."

I almost drop the phone as I stare at Cassius in the mirror, shocked at the suddenness of everything. When I put the phone to my ear and move into the changing room, Sargent answers, his voice deep and gruff.

"This better not be bad news, Cassius, I've had my quota for today."

Well... shit.

"It's me. Sorry, I left my phone at home," I explain before he can ask.

"Tempest," he replies, surprised. "It's good to hear your voice."

"You too, Sarge." I smile, twiddling my hair around my finger as I lean against the wall of the changing room. "How have you been?"

He hesitates and I wonder what he's hiding. "Good. Nothing to report."

There's a long pause before he asks, "Is everything okay?"

Deciding not to push the issue I get to the point of the conversation. "I'm leaving with Cassius on Thursday."

"Thursday? So soon?" His tone is cautious, I can't read it to understand how he feels about that.

"Yeah, we just got confirmation a few hours ago."

"Well, be safe. Don't go anywhere alone. Okay?"

I nod though obviously he can't see me. "I miss you."

"Don't." His tone is clipped, it startles me. "Just, go do your thing. Good luck, have fun, goodbye and all that shit."

"Sarge..."

"No, Tempest. You made your choice. It's been weeks."

"Oh." I understand now. He's over it. He's over me. "Sorry, I just thought..."

He clears his throat. "I have to go. Safe travels. See you at Christmas maybe."

The line goes dead and I'm left staring at Cassius' phone, feeling the urge to cry.

"Are you ready?" Cassius calls a few minutes later.

I exit the changing room dressed in my normal clothes and hand him my new ones.

"What's wrong?"

I shake my head slowly. "Sargent's moved on, I shouldn't have called."

"He said that?" Why does he look so confused?

"He didn't have to."

"Come on. I'm hungry."

Suddenly I feel nothing but nausea. I knew it was inevitable. What did I expect? That he'd be pining over me?

My ideals are laughable. I'm romanticizing everything. I put too much into such a short relationship, a mistake I'll never be making again.

I just thought life would finally go my way.

My dad was a drunk and the truth is, he used to beat us all so hard my brother lost his sight in his right eye. Didn't stop him from becoming just like him though. When my dad beat him, he beat me. When my dad beat me, he also beat me. It wasn't all the time, just sometimes. Just like sometimes I'd find my brother standing over my bed, staring down at me as he masturbated.

I lived with it for years and I couldn't take it anymore. Enough was enough.

I didn't plan to kill them, I just wanted to make them stop. I didn't murder them in cold blood. I wanted them to think I was crazy, I thought if they thought that, then they'd leave me alone. The plan was to just make them sleep for a while. I wanted them to think I could do it any time I wanted.

I crushed up a ton of sleeping pills using my friend's grinder and mixed it into the gravy at dinner. Mum was working late and when she worked late, my brother did things to me and my dad didn't care.

I used too many sleeping pills and neither of them woke up.

At first, I ran, but eventually I was found and was absolved of all charges. Still, Mum didn't want me back and my foster families were terrified of me. I ended up on the streets and felt so guilty for the deaths I caused I promised to use my life to do better.

Maddox knows this about me. He was the first person I ever told and he was the first person who didn't judge me for it, or fear me, he simply held me.

I chose to put my trust in the right person, until his father. Maybe all of this pain is still part of my penance.

This pain is my punishment. I'll never be allowed happiness. I don't even deserve it.

Sargent

"What's that?" Maddox asks, pointing at the white bandage on my chest. "You okay?"

"New ink," I reply, chewing on a piece of jerky.

"Can I see?"

I shake my head. "Needs to heal a bit first. I'll show you tomorrow."

"Whatever." He taps away on his phone and sighs. "Tempest is leaving early in the morning. Are you coming to see her off?"

"Absolutely not."

"Why?"

"Because I don't want to."

He rolls his eyes. "Scared you'll cry?"

"I'm over it," I lie. I'm not over it. Not in the slightest. I can't say goodbye because watching her go will destroy me.

"You love her," Maddox states simply, grinning at me again. "I don't know how you don't know it, but you do."

"I don't love her, Maddox. Christ, she's half my age."

"Age is but a number when you got wicked chemistry."

"Suddenly you want me and Tempest together?"

He smiles genuinely. "I want you both to be happy and you make each other happy. Who cares about anything else?"

"I don't love her."

"Prove it."

"I will, by not seeing her off."

"That's just cruel."

I shrug, wincing when my tattoo gives a sting of protest. "It doesn't matter how either of us feel. We want completely different things."

"So?"

"So?" I question his question with the same question.

"You love her, she loves you, everything else will fall into place."

"You're as naïve as she is."

He laughs loudly. "Probably. What would you have done if she were pregnant?"

"I would have done the right thing and married her."

He rolls his eyes again. "You're an idiot and you're missing out. She's going to come back with another man on this trip and forget all about you. He's going to be younger, better looking, more adventurous..."

"Maddox," I warn, not needing the visuals of her with another man.

"But you're over her so you don't care."

"She's leaving in the morning, like you said. She can do as she pleases."

"Why are you being so stubborn?"

"Because I want her to be fucking happy!" I yell, slamming my hand on the counter between us. "Enough, Maddox. She's better off without me and you know it. We're too different and those differences will drive her to fucking depression and resentment like your mother."

"Whoa," he murmurs and blinks at me, astounded I just said how I'm really feeling. "It's not your fault Mom is the way she is. She's a bitch, she was like that before you came along. As for Tempest being miserable? She already is. The only time I've ever seen her truly let herself be happy is with you. That day on the beach... I've never heard her laugh like that before. Never seen her smile like that. She thinks a life of unhappiness is her penance for her past."

I hate that she feels that way and wonder why I never just asked her about her past. I guess I was worried if I brought it up it would bring her mood down. Tempest always seemed so at peace with me, so relaxed. I got the feeling she didn't get that often so I let her have it.

"Drop it, Maddox."

"Go to Africa with her. It's only for two months. I can handle things here."

"No."

"Dad..."

"I said no. Let her find happiness with somebody that can keep it long term. I'm a fleeting love for her. A stepping stone. She deserves so much more."

He blows out a breath and throws his hands up. "I tried.

You're being a fucking moron." Then he leaves the room, slamming the door behind him.

I'm doing the right thing.

A few hours later, I peel back the bandage from my chest. My left peck to be exact and unveil the words that are a glistening black scrawl.

I weep at mine unworthiness, that dare not offer
What I desire to give, and much less take
What I shall die to want.

When Maddox sees it soon after he laughs once and snaps. "You don't love her, Dad, really? Pretty sure that's a specific line from The Tempest. Coincidence? Me thinks not."

I don't love her. He's wrong.

I don't love her because love isn't a strong enough word.

Tempest

I became one of those flimsy teen girls last night when I checked my phone repeatedly. I couldn't sleep. I need to accept the fact he isn't coming to say goodbye.

The fact I'm leaving hasn't hit me yet, not even slightly.

Maddox is here, looking around nervously on the tarmac below the private jet that will be dropping Cassius, myself, and the rest of the team off in Pointe-Noire. We're going to be traveling in total for at least three days to get from LA to Central

Africa. It's around a twenty-five-hour flight with a couple of stops for fuel.

To say we're dedicated would be an understatement.

I hug his waist and rest my head on his shoulder.

"He's not coming, stop looking for him."

I feel him shake his head and hear him sigh. "He's an idiot, Pest. You can do better. I was wrong."

"It is what it is." I lean back so he can kiss my forehead and tears blur my eyes and his. "Look after yourself, stay out of trouble."

"You too. I want weekly emails or I'm coming to look for you." He hugs me again and we sway for a while. "I'm going to miss you."

"I'll be back before you know it, sleeping in a spare room of your massive house, eating my way through your food." I'm joking of course. When and if I come back, I'll be an independent woman. Maybe I'll even find a new love.

Anything is better than this gaping hole in my chest.

I'm not going to shut myself off from the world and the prospect of love because it hurts. I like the hurt because it comes after all of the happiness and the happiness is worth this. It really is. My time with Sargent was worth this.

"Time to board," Cassius says and Maddox steps away from me to hug Cassius.

"Keep her safe."

"I'll do my best," Cassius replies and winks at me.

"Back on the meal replacement bars. I don't know how I'm going to cope without chocolate," I mumble when one of the crew wanders past with a box full of silver packets ready to be distributed during the flight.

We're all allocated a certain amount of food each for our bags so nobody can take more than they need.

"I'll send you some when I can," Maddox promises but we both know it won't get there.

I take one last look around the busy airport as planes take off, people stand at the windows and other planes circle above waiting to land.

"I was expecting some kind of romantic ending," I say and then start laughing. "I thought he'd come running for me at the last minute, we'd kiss and say one last cliché goodbye and that would be that."

"I'll give him a hard time for it later."

"Don't. He's doing what's easy for him. I can't fault him for that." I hug my friend again and squeeze as hard as I can. "I'm going to miss you both. Tell him... tell him I'm not sad. That I get it and... yeah, just tell him that."

"I hate that he's done this."

"Don't. I get it. He can't say goodbye." I back away and move to the narrow metal steps leading up to the plane. "I'll see you soon."

"You better be back for Christmas!" he snaps.

"I'll do my best."

"Weekly emails, Pest!"

"I'll do my best," I repeat, smiling sadly now.

"Stay safe."

This time I whisper it, "I'll do my best." Then, with tears falling from my eyes, I head inside and find a seat before the rest of the team arrive and the plane begins to fill. I sit by the window, wiping under my eyes with a balled-up tissue. He didn't even come to say goodbye.

Sargent

My heart breaks when I see her tears. She's crying for me, of course she is. I don't know how I ever doubted her love for me or ever let her go.

I keep my cap low and my head down as I make my way to the seat beside her. She doesn't look up from the window until I'm sitting next to her and place my hand on hers.

Her questioning scowl becomes a smile of so much happiness and love.

I lace our fingers together, her warm hand heating me to my frosty heart.

"I'm sorry," I say quietly, bringing her knuckles to my lips. "We have approximately three minutes until this plane leaves. Tell me right now you can't forgive me and I'll get off and you'll never see me again. Tell me I still have a chance and I'll come with you and show you every day how much I love you and love being with you."

"There won't be mattresses," she sniffs, turning to face me.

"I know."

"No home comforts, no coffee, no tea after the first few weeks. No internet, electric, chocolate."

I smile softly. "Will there be you?"

"Yeah," she replies, biting her lip. Her gorgeous eyes glitter with excitement. "There will be me."

"And you'll give me a do-over?"

Tears come with her laughter as she unbuckles her belt and wraps her arms around my neck. "I'll give you a do-over."

"Then I'm going wherever you are."

When I kiss her she accepts it and returns it with equal passion. She tastes sweet and I wonder how I ever thought I could give this up.

"I'm making the selfish choice, Tempest. I'm keeping you even though it's probably not the right thing to do."

She shakes her head at me, looking amused. "I don't care, we'll take it one day at a time. Everything else can come as it comes."

"Finally." Cassius grins at us before taking the seat beside me. "I was wondering when you'd show up."

I grin and kiss her again.

"There's a stipulation to this though, Tempest. After this trip we have to go on a vacation of my choosing, with a pool, and a beach and waiters."

She laughs, throwing her head back with it. "Deal. One hundred percent that's a deal."

I kiss her again, swallowing her laughter as Cassius makes gagging noises beside me. That is until I kick him in the shin with the back of my heel.

"It's time for safety speeches," somebody calls from some-where on the plane.

"The things we do for love," I grumble, kissing her one last time. "If I die, it's on you."

"Not even funny, Sarge," she replies, slapping my chest directly over the tattoo I'll reveal to her later. For now, I'm going to sit back, relax, and enjoy these last few hours of electricity with Tempest. Soon it'll be sleeping bags and tents.

Maddox: Miss you both already. Look after her, Dad.
Sargent: That goes without saying.

THE END

ACKNOWLEDGEMENTS

Yasmin Alyssia, thank you so much for always being one of the first to offer aid. I don't know what I'd do without you.

Addi Whillock, you keep me sane yet amplify my insanity all at the same time. You get it.

Samantha Louise Heaney, Adriana Rizak Healing, the twat sisters who I don't know how to live without.

B.A.N.G. My favorite group on FB. Thank you for keeping my days full of laughter.

My kids, thank you for helping Mummy while she's working. You're incredible little babes. Even though I hope you never read this.

Momma G and Papa Rue, aka, Gina (Mummy) and Rue (Step-Daddy), thank you for having the kids during my signings, etc, and for everything else you do.

Siobhan, my sister, for having my daughter in return for me having your son. You owe me way more than I owe you but here's the mention you moan you never get. Yes, I know, I'm so funny.

Mary Murphy, my nan who is also one of my best friends and an amazing poet. I love you and you know it. See what I did there?

ABOUT THE AUTHOR

A. E. Murphy is the queen of sarcasm and satire, she likes long walks in the park, as much as ice cubes like to chill in a roasting oven.

She's effortlessly independent and so good at adulting it's unfair on the rest of the world. She only napped twice today and has only avoided the dishes for three days before making the child slaves do them this morning.

Winning!

Her favourite hobby is writing, her worst hobby is reading through that writing.

Also, she has ~~two~~ three cats that carry toys to the top of the stairs and drop them down so they can chase them. They do this repeatedly in the middle of the night.

Who cares if she has work the next morning?

Not the cats, that's for sure.

And if it's not the cats doing the waking, it's the toddler crawling into bed with her and pulling individual hairs from her scalp with pudgy little fingers for comfort.

This is likely why she's in a constant state of grump unless there's chocolate and coffee.

P.S. Please leave feedback, if not on the book then on this ridiculous bio she wrote herself. It's the least you can do seeing as she'll forever talk in the third person now.

Alex loves her readers. Alex says thank you. Alex smiles.

Contact

Website
aemurphyauthor.com

Email
a.e.murphy@hotmail.com

facebook.com/a.e.murphy.autho

twitter.com/A_E_Murphy

ALSO BY THE AUTHOR

The Little Bits Series

A Little Bit of Crazy

A Little Bit of Us

A Little Bit of Trouble

A Little Bit of Truth

The Distraction Trilogy

Distraction

Destruction

Distinction

The Broken Trilogy

Broken

Connected

Forever

A Broken Story

Disconnected (Dillan)

Standalone Novels

Masked Definitions

Sweet Demands Trilogy

Lockhart

Lockdown

Unlocked

31080604R00159

Printed in Poland
by Amazon Fulfillment
Poland Sp. z o.o., Wrocław